VISA TO LIMBO

VISA
TO
LIMBO

William Haggard

WALKER AND COMPANY
NEW YORK

VISA TO LIMBO

ONE

Rifai sat in his fine veranda waiting for his martyr's crown. He thought of himself as a civilized man and as such he was suspicious of violence. Alas that there were others who weren't, like that swaggering mountebank ranting interminably, going to New York with a gun in his trouser belt, posing as an unquestioned leader when all he was was an upstart bullyboy. Rifai held him in a blazing contempt for Rifai was a man with a practical vision. But different from most of these since he saw his disadvantage clearly. The influence of that clown was diminishing but it hadn't yet entirely faded. Others before Rifai had been realists. All had been denounced with fury; all had ignominiously failed; and two had died unpleasant deaths.

The Israelis, in this occupied town, had behaved with a scrupulous moderation, though the Captain of Israeli police was now the town's effective master. Rifai hadn't challenged him — why indeed do so? This ancient, sleepy town was negotiable. It wasn't in any area which the Israelis could claim was strategically vital, no part of the defensible frontiers which the state of Israel was defensibly claiming. So sooner or later they'd trade it away for something which they really wanted.

Then why change from acceptance to open rebellion? There was only one but a very good reason. To bring his vision from the mists to reality he needed that martyr's crown as his passport. He could go to Alidra tomorrow quite freely but he wouldn't have a reputation, nothing to build on, no men to follow him. He'd be just another refugee and he needed much more than that to achieve his dream.

His and that Israeli Admiral's. Rifai had several Israeli friends but the Admiral was by far the closest.

And now chance had turned his card up clearly; the affair of those ridiculous settlers. And ridiculous they had been — no threat. There was water in this town from famous wells, even enough for a few bananas, notoriously the most thirsty of fruit, but there wasn't a margin for further settlement; and with world opinion the way it was the Israelis wouldn't dare risk displacements. These intruders had been right wing students, intellectuals making the dubious point that the whole of the biblical land of Palestine was theirs for whatever use they selected. They'd arrived with their tents and a little water; they had pitched their tents and there they had squatted.

That was the word — they'd simply squatted. Without serious, planned official backing they hadn't had a hope in hell, and that backing had been notably absent. To make anything like a serious settlement, they'd need housing, machinery, food until their crops came in. And, above all things, ample water. But they had only what they'd brought in drums. When that was gone they'd have to go. It was a meaningless gesture and therefore stupid. Rifai had quietly shrugged it off.

But the men of the town had seen it otherwise. Less sophisticated than their town's cool mayor they'd gone down to these squalid tents and wrecked the site.

Rifai recalled the affair with distaste. There'd been blind violence of the kind he detested.

He had gone with the angry men of his township and they had beaten settlers and settlement into the ground. Rifai had expected a certain disturbance for he knew his own people better than most, their virtues and also their crippling weaknesses, but he hadn't expected fire and blood. Tents had been fired and men had danced round them, thrusting their inmates back with ancient swords. The Occupiers had stripped them of firearms but had left them their ancestral cutlery which they prized as they prized their women's virtue. Children had been maimed and disfigured and Rifai had ordered the horror to stop. Perhaps he would have been obeyed and perhaps, in the reek of alien blood, his orders would have gone unheeded. What happened was that a squatter had brought a gun. He drew it and missed but the damage was done. After that it was very much better not thought of.

When the armed police arrived they behaved impeccably, refraining from fire, using butts and truncheons. They were carefully picked men and they knew their business. In five minutes it was all over, finished. The officer got on his blower for ambulances. He made no arrests on the Arab side.

This frightened Rifai much more than if he had. There was a pattern for these affairs and a precedent. It mightn't be the police next day but soldiers, and they'd have high explosives. . . . A charge inside each wall of a house, a bang and the roof came down on a ruin. It was brutal but competent field engineering. They cleared the houses before they blew them, but their owners would be homeless migrants, dependent on relatives poor already.

But it was police who were coming this morning, not soldiers. Rifai had been warned they were on their way for their Captain had sent him a courteous message. He'd be calling at nine o'clock precisely and would be grateful to be received for a chat.

So now Rifai sat and waited quietly, looking around the wide veranda. Its roof was supported by ageless columns pillaged from a neighbouring ruin by ancestors with an eye for elegance. Rifai had been under pressure to give them back — they were restoring the ruin to show to tourists — but he had no intention whatever of doing so. His veranda was unique in the town. It was alien to all Arab building but what his forbears had achieved by accident was something quite close to a classical stoa. Most of antiquity's races had passed this way. Nobody had unquestioned title but every man believed he held it.

As he waited he made a mental balance sheet, his assets against his liabilities. Of the latter only one really counted, that he lacked the label of loyal Resister. Well, he'd have that in an hour or two; and on the assets side he had plenty to play with. He'd been sent to an English school in Amman, for his father had been mayor before him, his family was rich and established, and you couldn't get far in the outside world without an international language upon your tongue. Then two years in England at engineering. He hadn't stayed to take his final degree, for his father had died and they'd called him home, but he'd easily find a job in Alidra. Alidra was where his future lay, his future and his vision's too. All he needed was that martyr's crown.

4

And so far the omens were better than good, for he knew what the Captain of police would want. He'd want to take him into Israel proper where his superiors would be polite but firm. At the lowest they'd want an explanation.

And Rifai wasn't going, he meant to resist. If necessary with the violence he hated.

He looked round the clearing outside his house. To call it a square would be overstatement — Arab builders had seldom thought of squares — but undeniably it was open ground and the men of the town had begun to collect on it. For he'd passed out the news of the Captain's call and a hint that it would not be routine. He wanted publicity, all he could garner; he wanted events to be *coram populo*. Then they'd promptly go round the Arab world. Rifai the quiet mayor of this ancient town, suspect perhaps of a certain indifference, would be suddenly an established hero. People would listen and men would follow him. He needed them or his plan wouldn't work.

Rifai looked at the gathering men of the town. They were hostile and surly but silent and frightened. They knew what they stood to lose if they played it wrong.

The commander of the police saluted and he did it without a hint of irony. He addressed Rifai in courteous Arabic, wishing him all the blessings of heaven, but was punctilious not to use the word Allah. In the mouth of a Jew that was impermissible. He concluded:

'I should like to speak with you.'

Rifai didn't answer; he stared down in hostility.

'There'd be advantages in a word in private.'

'I do not wish to speak with barbarians.'

The Captain pretended to misunderstand him. 'I'm

sorry my Arabic isn't good.' In fact it was very good indeed. 'You would prefer another language? English perhaps? I know you speak it.'

Rifai said in excellent English: 'Go. Leave us in peace to mourn our freedom.'

'But it isn't quite as easy as that.' The Captain was still calm and conciliatory. 'There was an attack on our people and several were injured. I know that they had no right to be there. Their action was both wrong and illegal, which aren't always quite the same things in Israel, but you're the mayor of this town and whom else can I talk to?'

Rifai stayed silent and the Captain said quietly:

'I come in peace.'

'Then go to your grave with our hate to haunt you.'

The Captain lit a cigarette, asking formal permission before he did so. When he had smoked perhaps a half he said, and he had gone back to Arabic:

'Your Honour, you are not a realist.' This above all things was what Rifai was, so he looked at the growing crowd again. It had swelled and there were even some women, the audience was in, the curtain up. It was time for his scene. He began to play it.

He rose from his chair and pointed dramatically; he began to abuse the Captain obscenely. He cast doubt upon the Captain's ancestry, graver doubt upon his mother's virtue. As for himself his children were changelings, strays smuggled into a woman's bed since her husband had been an impotent pederast. He went on in this vein for some time and he watched the crowd. They were lapping it up with a practised relish, for in this sort of insult the Arabic language was unmatched by any other on earth.

The Captain stood and took it in silence. It wasn't discipline which reined his temper but something much more powerful — indifference. The words rolled off him like rain from a greenhouse. None of his men had even smiled. Those who knew Arabic thought it childish, and those who did not were plainly bored. They had seen this before and it cooked no dinners.

The Captain interrupted in English. 'If you won't talk sensibly I'll be forced to arrest you.'

'Arrest me then. Torture me. Do as you will.'

There wasn't the slightest risk of torture. He was the mayor of an occupied town. He was privileged.

The Captain looked at his watch and shrugged, then he looked at the crowd. It was edging in menacingly. His sergeant saw this too and asked:

'One or two over their heads?'

'Certainly not, it's against the rules.' (In this, though the Captain didn't know it, he was following standard western practice.) 'But take a quick look round for cameras. You never know when some American tourist won't be hiding behind a tree with a camera and we don't want this silly affair in *Time*.'

The sergeant went off and returned in five minutes. 'I didn't see any camera.'

'Right.'

Rifai overheard him and hid a smile. The last act of this charade was imminent. The Captain said: 'You are under arrest.'

Rifai had come down from the raised veranda, facing the Captain in open ground. The more that was seen and heard the better.

'I deny your authority. I deny your right in this land. It is ours.'

There was a murmur from the crowd but no more.

'I'm not an international lawyer, I'm a policeman and I have my orders.' He looked at Rifai; he was summing him up. 'I hope you're coming quietly.'

'Never.' Rifai's voice had risen so the back row could hear it. 'I protest. I will give my blood——'

'Oh, stuff it.' The Captain was a professional policeman and he hated the least hint of heroics; he stood waiting for Rifai's next move but he was balanced on the balls of his feet.

Rifai took a clumsy swing at him. The Captain ducked the swing and smiled.

'That will get you nowhere, friend.'

There'd been a murmur from the crowd again but it hadn't been one of entire approval. It knew a fight when it saw it and this wasn't a good one.

Rifai stood locked in a bleak uncertainty. Anything approaching a brawl would be something he'd detest till he died, but that sound from the crowd had warned him fairly. He had to show action and show it quickly... The Militant, the local hero. The unthinking, uncounting Palestinian Resister.

He was none of these things, he despised them all equally. He was a visionary with a practical plan.

He sighed but he rushed the Captain creditably. The Captain hit him twice but mercifully. Rifai fell down and began to writhe. The crowd shouted but made no move to help him. These were policemen and armed, not young students and children.

The Captain said: 'Pick him up.' His men did so. They carried him to a truck and put him in. They weren't gentle but nor were they stupidly rough with him.

They lodged him not in a common cell but in a comfortable room with air-conditioning. The windows were barred and the door was kept locked but he wasn't molested in any way. He was invited to choose his own food and did so.

He waited patiently since he was sure what would happen. It would take them a couple of days to decide, the politicians who ran this frenetic country, but in practice they had only two options and Rifai had no doubt of which option they'd choose. They could put him on trial and expose the story or they could push him across an Arab frontier. But the former held too many risks to be practical. The story of his heroic resistance (he frowned in distaste as the phrase occurred to him) would go round the Arab world on the grapevine but must at all costs not reach the western Press. Especially at this particular moment when the western Press was largely pro Arab and what wasn't was balanced too finely for comfort. So they'd conduct him to a post and let him go.

Rifai knew exactly which state he'd make for. He would go to Alidra since Alidra had oil. He had a knowledge of civil engineering and he'd find himself work without much difficulty. Dozens like himself had done so, for the Alidrans were a backward people and they couldn't run their oil alone.

Nor their land, once fruitful, now dying shamefully. Rifai coveted it with unceasing passion since with it he could reverse recent history. Not strutting at the United Nations, not hijackings and bombings of school-children, but a solid and lasting work of resettlement. Of course he'd have to pay a price, the price of the men who would make that possible, the experts in agronomy, the men who would drill for water, not for oil. The Admiral would ask a price for their labours and that price would be a little oil. Rifai was perfectly willing to pay it. There were twin pillars to his majestic dream.

So he was going to turn the tide back finally, with land and a little help from the Admiral. The Admiral was an Israeli hawk but a necessary ally too. Uneasy bedfellows? Yes, very much so. But *realpolitik* had its own imperatives.

TWO

Colonel Charles Russell, lately head of the Security Executive, had decided that he would lunch at his club. The food had deteriorated but the wine was still excellent and he hadn't been there for several weeks. He might meet a friend or a bore might hook him, but with bores his technique was both bland and decisive. He could get rid of them without putting their backs up, and this was a talent not all men shared. Nor that for a quiet but ruthless action. Employed to run the Security Executive he had done so to his country's advantage. Now he was in deserved retirement, but the aura of an unquestioned authority had stayed with him whether he liked it or not. Beneath the cool and easy manner was a man who had fought on Security's battlefield where rules were unknown and the struggle merciless.

He was shutting the door of his first floor flat when he heard footsteps on the stairs above him. A man's voice called: 'Colonel Russell. Wait please.'

Charles Russell turned and looked up the staircase. A man and a woman were coming down it. The man was called the Young Sheikh and Russell knew him. The woman he had never met but had heard of her existence more than once. 'Good morning,' he said to the Sheikh politely.

'I'm delighted to catch you. I have to go back to

Alidra this evening and I wouldn't have liked to go without saying goodbye.'

'I'm very sorry indeed to hear it.' This wasn't politeness but simple truth. The Young Sheikh, or sometimes the Prince more formally, had the flat above Russell's as London *pied-à-terre* and they'd formed more than the casual acquaintance of neighbours. Russell looked at his watch. 'You're lunching out? Come in and have a drink before you go.'

The Young Sheikh looked at the woman, who nodded. He introduced her. 'Mrs Lynne Hammer. A friend of mine for a long time now.' It was very urbanely done and the woman smiled. Russell opened the door of his flat and they all went in.

He inquired what Lynne Hammer would drink, which was gin, and handed her escort a whisky and soda. He knew the Prince could trace descent from the Prophet and in Alidra he was strictly orthodox, but in the western world he would take a drink provided no other Muslim were present, and he would do so without fuss or apology. He didn't claim as another once had that he was so holy that alcohol turned to water the instant it passed his sacred lips. He drank with enjoyment in moderation, one of the good things of life he relished but was prepared to forgo where it wasn't acceptable. He deplored that necessity but he didn't complain of it. He was a pragmatist and Charles Russell liked him. In a real sense they were birds of a feather.

Lynne Hammer said: 'Your very good health.'

'The same to you.' Russell looked at her shrewdly. He didn't veil his inspection, an open compliment, since he'd judged that she'd take no offence whatever if his expression should tell her he'd placed her perfectly. Evidently she was the Young Sheikh's mistress. No doubt she would have a comfortable flat but it wouldn't be flashy or tiresomely grand. The Young Sheikh was very rich indeed and would shortly be rich beyond any man's dream, but he detested ostentation heartily.

She said with a smile: 'You'll know me again.'

'I've been staring? It's a very bad habit.'

'There are several ways of indulging it.'

'Yes.' He knew what she meant, she was flattered, not angry. And indeed she was well worth a man's attention. Forty, perhaps, or a little more, full-bodied but a long way from stout. No doubt she wore something other than underclothes but whatever it was it was unobtrusive. His eyes were grey and bold and steady.

Unexpectedly she dropped them quickly.

The Young Sheikh said in the beautiful English which he'd learnt at his London school and Harvard:

'It's really very distressing indeed. I had hoped to stay here two months at least, but my uncle is going downhill rather fast. He's been dying for some time, as you'll know, but the latest news is very bad. There's been some sort of crisis — I've got to go to him.'

'I'm sorry,' Russell said. He meant it. This heir to an unwanted throne was no playboy, not a man to duck duty. He liked the west, he enjoyed its freedoms, but he'd go back to his oil-drunk half-barbarous sheikhdom simply because he'd been born to rule it. That was a duty and so inescapable. Russell looked at him, this time without staring. He was evidently some kind of Semite, but many men would have tossed a coin to decide whether he was Arab or Jew. He was handsome in his Arab way — beautifully barbered beard and fine features — but it wasn't his looks which earned Russell's approval. This was a man with an obligation; he'd discharge it although he didn't desire to.

There was an unexpected noise in the street and the three of them went to Russell's window. There were twenty or thirty men and women shouting slogans and waving furious fists. It was a demonstration, though not a big one, and all of them wore the demo's uniform, the men shoulder-length hair and tinted glasses, the women jeans and oversize sweaters. They'd been hired from an agency, two pounds a head, for these were the rooters, not the organized heavies. The heavies got rather more than two pounds. In the front was a banner, crudely painted.

FREE KUNN AT ONCE

'What a very odd name.'

'Who is he anyway?'

Lynne Hammer shrugged.

The Sheikh had gone back to his chair and his whisky. 'It's a misliteration,' he said indifferently. He pronounced it in Arabic and Russell frowned.

'But he isn't in England — the Israelis caught him. They'll almost certainly jail him too.'

'In my view,' the Sheikh said, 'perfectly properly.'

'Then why is that rabble outside in the street?'

'Because they know I detest all terrorists. Or rather the people who hired them do.'

'Which implies the hirers know you're here.'

'They've been following me about for days. They pester me but they don't risk violence.'

'Don't you have, well, some sort of escort?'

The Sheikh said with a hint of asperity: 'I'm going to spend the rest of my life under some sort of guard or at least surveillance. I'd prefer not to start until I'm obliged to.' He returned to the window and looked out coolly. A bottle came up but it missed the glass. It broke on the brickwork, falling down to the basement. He came back to his chair and Russell gave him more whisky. 'Palestinians,' he said with a cold contempt.

'You don't seem to care for them much.'

The Sheikh laughed. 'You have a gift for understatement, Colonel, and since I lack it I will not compete. As a people I entirely mistrust them and their Organization fills me with horror. It's bloodthirsty and ineffective to boot. I sympathize with what they want — I'm an Arab, though of a different sort — but they're destroying our common cause by stupidity.'

Charles Russell considered; he didn't like what had happened. If the Sheikh left now there'd be some sort of incident, and an incident outside Russell's door would bring the Press swarming down on his peace like bees. He said at length:

'What time is your plane?'

'At five this evening. Check in at four.'

'Then I think you'd better stay for luncheon.'

The Prince rose at once. 'I'm not scared of hired children.'

'No,' Russell said, 'I can see you're not. But I happen to live here. You do not.'

The Sheikh thought it over. 'I owe an apology. We accept your most generous invitation.' He thought again. 'And after luncheon?'

'The police will have moved them on as a nuisance, or if they haven't I still have a certain influence. I think

I can promise unhindered passage provided you do nothing untimely.'

They had omelettes and cheese and two bottles of Burgundy. Russell's housekeeper made omelettes well and the Burgundy was Aloxe Corton. Lynne Hammer was very quiet indeed but the wine had warmed the Arab's stomach and he unbent from his race's natural reserve.

'You are wondering what all this is about, and I owe an explanation anyway.'

'I'm not pressing you,' Charles Russell said.

'I know. If you did I wouldn't say a thing.' He accepted a final glass of wine. 'In one way it's very simple indeed and in another it's a mess of intrigue.' He drank some more wine and nodded appreciatively. 'The simple part is my hatred of terrorists, but it goes a good deal deeper than that. My uncle whom I shall shortly succeed is hardly famous for his liberal leanings and Palestinians are notably left of liberal. But we can't run our oil without Palestinians—they're much brighter than our own poor people, better educated and incidentally more treacherous. So we bring them in because we must, but my uncle's been very sparing with citizenship. He's learnt the lesson of what they tried in Jordan, of what they nearly brought off in Lebanon too till the Syrians cut them down to size. Some people think he's been far too hospitable but he isn't going to be taken over. Nor, for that matter, am I, I assure you. So naturally my House is hated.' He used the word without hint of pomposity, smiling because there wasn't a better one.

'A difficult situation.'

'Very.'

'I don't envy you.'

'I don't envy myself.'

Coffee came in and Charles Russell's best brandy. Russell and Lynne drank black coffee, straight, but the Prince had eaten with Russell before and his house-keeper liked him and knew what pleased. She brought him coffee in a small brass pot, unbelievably strong and almost solid with sugar. She poured it out with a flourish; he thanked her gracefully.

Over it he relaxed some more. 'So you see I shan't be exactly popular when my uncle goes to join the houris. He has the reputation of a pious boob and certainly he's excessively pious, but "boob" is his deliberate cover. Every Arab ruler needs a cover — he wouldn't last a month without it. So he's training up our own people quietly, and when he's done it he'll throw the hotheads out. Or I'll do the same thing and the hotheads know it. Back they'll go to their camps and to unemployment. Naturally they do not love me. They call me a traitor but the insult runs off me. I'm as good an Arab as they are — better — but I was schooled in the west and it taught me expediency. The hotheads think I'm as wet as a dishcloth.'

'The hotheads may get a surprise.'

'They will. But there's another thing that's running against me, the matter of Oceanic Oil.'

'Which holds the concession which has never been tampered with.'

'Why should we tamper? It serves us well. But Oceanic is a Jewish company. They have a Gentile board as a convenient front, but the real control, the say-so, the guts of them, is as Jewish as a trainload of rabbis.'

'Does your uncle know that?'

'It's hard to say. It's always hard to say what he knows. I would guess that he does but he doesn't care. It would be different if they were actively Zionists — sent money or arms or men into Israel. But Oceanic is strictly Brooklyn Jewish right down to their hiding the household *mezuzah*. They're doing very nicely, thank you, and foreign adventures don't attract them. I have the advantage of spending three years in America, and though the Jewish vote can swing an election, by no means all Jews are actively Zionist. But my Palestinian brethren think otherwise. Of course it's an over-simplification but it's also another black mark against me. If I don't throw Oceanic out I'll be just another lukewarm oil sheikh. And I'm not lukewarm in any way. It's simply that political ends are mostly achieved by political means, and though violence is a political means uncontrolled violence is self-defeating.'

'You're a philosopher in your way.'

'I'm sensible.' The Young Sheikh went to the window again. 'They've gone,' he announced.

'Would you like me to ring for a taxi?'

'Thank you.'

When the taxi arrived they all went down to it. There wasn't a protester in sight. They had melted away like snow in June when the time which they had been hired for was over. The banner lay in the gutter, abandoned. It hadn't been theirs and was therefore expendable.

Lynne Hammer said: 'A delightful luncheon.'

'I hope we meet again.'

'We shall.'

Some spark had passed between them. Both knew it.

The Sheikh put her into the taxi politely, then held out his hand to Russell. 'Goodbye'. He was still wearing his beautiful English clothes, still speaking his almost accentless English, but in some way which Charles Russell could not define he'd suddenly become a Prince. An alien Prince, a Prince of the Arabs.

'But must it be goodbye?' Russell said.

'I'm very much afraid it must. One part of my life is over now. I enjoyed it and I regret its loss. Another less pleasant will start in a day or two.'

'God go with you,' Russell said.

'And with you.'

In the taxi Mrs Lynne Hammer was silent. So was the Sheikh, though for different reasons, for he had noticed the black Mercedes behind them. He'd been followed before and it didn't much trouble him, since if they got him it would not be in London. He wondered but without much interest who the men in the car behind would be. Probably el Hakim's hirelings. The Old Sheikh had been excessively hospitable for he knew what el Hakim stood for and planned, but the doctor was an excellent chess player and in Alidra such men were very rare.

The Admiral sat in his modest apartment, one in a block of the warm local stone which they'd built with an astonishing speed since Jerusalem had been reunited. By crossing a road and then climbing a mound he could look down on the great mosque of Omar, its gilded dome glinting in evening sunlight. For a man who had once been a politician the site was a rather surprising choice, far from the intrigue and bustle of a political life which had now discarded him. His neighbours were doctors or academics, and with the former he had little in common. With the academics he had nothing at all. But his new wife had liked it and that had decided. In any case he knew that in politics he'd been used as a front and had therefore failed. It was better to live away from the hubbub in a peace which his ripening years made seemly. And this Mount on which he lived had been liberated: its soil under his feet had been bought with blood. Israel had started that war? An impertinent lie. The Admiral would have agreed with Taine that the men who could be said to start wars were the men who had made those wars inevitable. He had lost an arm in bitter battle; he was sixty-three but hale and vigorous. Indeed he'd just remarried successfully.

He'd come to Israel as little more than a boy, going first to a *kibbutz*, then to fighting. First one enemy and then another, a soldier when there'd been no navy, then he'd transferred and made his name. He had risen to Father Figure, a Hero, then been pushed into politics not too successfully. Naturally he'd gone in with Herut, but even there his views had been thought extreme.

But he believed they weren't extreme — only sensible. If his country had any future at all it must survive by its sword and not by diplomacy. He'd been worried in the Yom Kippur war for he'd seen signs of what he considered degeneracy. But the expresso children had not been degenerate. They had sprung from their cafés, their speculations and theories, and inflicted on the eternal enemy a defeat which would surely have been the final one if America hadn't stopped them dead. America wasn't really their friend, America put America first. Not that he blamed her but there it was. To rely on her was a very great foolishness.

He went into the communal garden — succulents and flowering shrubs. The sun was getting hotter now and the man who was waiting was fanning his face.

'Good morning, Admiral.'

'Good morning, friend.' Surprisingly they were talking Polish. 'You have a message for me?'

'Yes, sir, I have. Rifai has made it.'

'Made it to Alidra?'

'Yes.'

'That,' the Admiral said, 'is good.'

'I will arrange a channel at once.'

'That is better. Is there anything else?'

'For the moment, no.'

'Then please keep me in touch.'

'I understand.'

He went back into the flat and to breakfast, the enormous Israeli breakfast he loved. His young wife brought it in with a smile. He dispatched it with an evident relish and she, who was happily pregnant, did the same. Later she slipped away to her chores.

He began to polish a coin with a washleather cloth, for besides his reputation as Hero he had another and considerable fame as a numismatist of the highest class. But this morning his collection betrayed him; he wasn't in the mood for pottering.

He picked up a book with a certain reluctance since he wasn't a man who cared much for books. It was openly Arab propaganda but that wasn't the reason it frayed his nerves. They had a perfect right to state their case and he wouldn't have suppressed this book even if he'd had power to do so. But the book was lacking in mental discipline and without it propaganda lost impact. A phrase like 'inalienable rights', for instance. What rights had ever in fact been inalienable? And what was this about *ashkenazim*? He was one himself, he'd been born in a ghetto, and he wasn't ashamed of his background and blood. But the author equated the word with brigand: Israel could only hope to be peaceful when the *sephardim*, the oriental Jews, came to power and gave their country away.

The Admiral chuckled. They wouldn't do that. This intelligent but blinkered lawyer had got it rather seriously wrong.

He took a tray from a cabinet, fiddling with coins again, but he couldn't relax, his sharp brain was in overdrive.

What a collective fool the western world was! Couldn't it see what was under its nose, that the men with the guns were a very poor bet, but that others more reliable were there for the intelligent using?

Men like Rifai who was now in Alidra.

For Fatah and all its murderous offspring he felt a fighting man's deep and complete contempt. Put them behind artillery, preferably in a concrete bunker, and they'd fire away like proper gunners till a counter-battery dropped on their range. Then they'd depart to cook a meal. Or they'd tear around with recoilless rifles, preferably in a jeep for mobility, blasting away at whatever moved and as often as not at whatever did not, but when it came to the bloody business of street fighting somehow they didn't seem so keen. And look how they had bungled Jordan. Black September indeed! The Admiral wrinkled his nose disdainfully.

They'd come in as honoured refugees and they'd repaid it by trying to take over their hosts. They'd had an excellent chance of doing so too. Just a little more patience, political know-how. But no, they'd forced the issue arrogantly, inviting a tank battle to settle it. Where they'd been whipped in their borrowed armour like dogs. And when the locust horde had descended on Lebanon the story had been the same but worse. The Syrians had pulled their punches since they hadn't needed to punch their real weight, but they'd cleaned up these so-called fighting men as they'd have cleaned up an unruly Sunday school.

These reflections had cleared his morning choler, and he thought again of Rifai and their project. There were others like him too, though not many. Not many yet — they didn't dare. To be branded as a collaborator could earn a man worse than social ostracism, so Rifai had been forced to play it clever, to build himself up as a local martyr. He'd be accepted in Alidra unquestioningly and he'd know how he must use that acceptance.

To his people's advantage, to the Admiral's too. Rifai wanted land, the Admiral oil. Oil should be his final gift to the state to which he had given his life. Lack of it was the ball and chain round his dependant country's felon feet, but with it they could shape their own future without looking over an anxious shoulder at a continent whose charity kept them alive.

So Rifai was in Alidra now . . .

Charles Russell's doorbell rang unexpectedly and he opened with some surprise to Lynne Hammer. 'You don't mind?' she asked.

'I'm delighted. Come in.'

He put her in a comfortable chair and inquired if she would still drink gin.

'I'll have whisky if I may. I need it.'

He gave her whisky on the rocks: she drank half of it. Charles Russell said, trying to ease her tension:

'Seeing people off is hell.'

'Seeing people off indeed! I'll never see the Sheikh again.'

'I'm afraid he was trying to tell me the same.' He let her finish her whisky and gave her another. 'Would you care to tell me all about it?'

'That's what I came for, you know. A good listener.'

'I'm not always that, but talk just the same.'

'I met him in America. I was nursing in a New York clinic.' She looked down at her ample but disciplined figure. 'I was slimmer then but not very much.'

'I like you very well as you are.'

'That's fine. If I were a man I'd like a woman who was one. The Sheikh felt the same — we went click at once. Would you care to hear?'

'I would very much.' Charles Russell meant it. He was finding this woman more than interesting, difficult to place, exciting. Even her speech was a challenge to label. Basically it was still mid-Western, but overlaid by the accent and sometimes the idiom of a woman who had lived for years with a man who had learnt his English in England.

'All right,' she said, 'here it comes if you want it.' She lit a cigarette, collecting her thoughts. 'I'm quite an Old American really. My family came from the South originally and there's a tradition we owned a grand plantation like something out of Joseph Hergesheimer. But I suspect we were really just poor whites because when Lincoln signed the Homestead Act we promptly moved north-west to the plains. And there we still are, not rich and not poor. My parents gave me a good education, and off I went to nurse the sick, which was the only way I could think of then to escape from small town life in the sticks. And I surely did escape, yes sir! I was attractive to men and I liked them too, and you've no idea how that helps on the nursing ladder. I moved steadily east till I got to New York in a very expensive clinic indeed, and there one day I met the Sheikh. They'd brought him in with a boil on his toe, something any English doctor would have treated at home as a matter of course, but American doctors aren't like that, they hospitalize you at the drop of a hat. So there the Sheikh was with nothing much wrong with him and some hotel doctor laughing his head off since he'd probably be taking a cut from the clinic. That's wildly unethical, even illegal, but it happens every day of the year.' She finished her cigarette, lit another. 'So we cleaned the Sheikh up in three or four days, but in that time quite a lot had happened. He was very attractive and I knew he was rich or he wouldn't have been in that clinic at all. In any case I was getting bored with it. So when he made me a proposition I jumped at it. He took me down to Acapulco and we've stayed together ever since. What I like about men you can probably guess and next to that I like them tolerant. For an Arab my Sheikh was amazingly tolerant and on top of that he was generous too. So it's natural we stayed together successfully.'

Charles Russell allowed a smile, relaxing. He was

beginning to like Lynne Hammer a lot. She had the directness which drew the sting from materialism and an agreeably earthy view of sex. She had the candour of the professional mistress. Without it she couldn't have lived with grace. She was saying now:

'So you see I like men.'

It was the clearest and least encumbered of openings but he wasn't quite ready to march right through it. 'Tell me more about the Sheikh,' he said.

'He isn't strictly that yet but he very soon will be. His uncle is dying and that's why he's gone. And he's going to have a life he'll hate.'

'I'm very much afraid you're right.'

'So I met him in America and we've been like this for a good few years. After his astonishing tolerance I liked best that he was always honest. He couldn't marry me and he told me why. He has a wife under Islamic law but so far she's only given him daughters. Sooner or later he'll take another but that other isn't going to be me. An infidel American woman.... It would tear Alidra to pieces overnight.'

He didn't answer that; it was obvious.

'But that isn't why I'm feeling bloody. I like men and I don't come alive without one, but I don't have to marry them all. Far from it. What hurts is that I'll never see him.'

'Perhaps he'll be able to slip away——'

'Oh no, he won't do that. He can't. He'll be up to his neck in intrigue and politics.'

'Again I'm afraid that's also true.'

'And it isn't as though he loved me madly. He liked me but he was also an Arab. No Arab entirely falls for a woman, he would think it rather unmanly to do so.

But as a master he was almost perfect.'

Charles Russell was surprised. 'A master?'

'Since I was his mistress why not "master"? And as that he had great style and panache. He didn't rush out and buy me diamonds whenever we'd had a good night together, but if I wanted to do something foolish like that trip to Bankok I'd set my heart on he'd cancel all dates and fly next day.'

'I couldn't afford that,' Russell said.

'Nor could I then, but I could today. He's really left me extremely comfortable. The next man I take won't have to keep me.' She changed gear and he saw it was done deliberately. They were going a little too fast to be seemly. 'So now my not-so-romantic Sheikh, my practical, generous, civilized Prince, has been swallowed by a life he'll detest.' She looked up with an unexpected sharpness. 'How much do you know of the Middle East?'

'Only what I read in the newspapers. I'm retired so I don't see the real hard news.'

'But you know that Alidra has oil?'

'Of course.'

'The Israelis would like that oil.'

'No doubt. But the slightest move to take it over and the super powers would for once act together.'

'A sound judgement, sir, but superficial.'

'What do you mean by superficial?' Charles Russell sounded a little dry.

'It isn't just Arabs fighting Israelis. All Israelis want much the same thing, security, but they're divided on the best way to get it.'

'I knew there was more than one party in Israel.'

'One of them is pretty extreme.'

He was interested. 'Please go on.'

'Maybe I'll tell you later, maybe I won't. It depends how things develop.'

'Understood.'

Russell mixed more drinks and sat down again quietly. He'd been surprised but was now on familiar ground. Mrs Lynne Hammer was in his own business. Without changing his voice he asked her simply:

'Whom do you work for?'

She didn't flinch. 'I worked for Oceanic Oil.' Charles Russell hadn't changed his voice and Lynne Hammer didn't change her expression. 'But naturally I told my master.'

'You told the Sheikh?'

'Of course I did.'

'Didn't he throw you out?'

'Why should he? In point of fact he laughed for three minutes. I thought he was going to have a stroke. It was silly, you see, and my dear friend knew it. It was International Corporation playing at spies and making a balls of it. They had nothing to fear from my very dear friend — they needed him but he needed them equally. So I took their money and the Sheikh shared the joke with me. Every quarter I got in touch with a contact and assured him the heir apparent was sound. For that they paid me absurdly well and that money is now in their own fat company. If you press me I'm really quite a rich woman.'

'Not only rich,' he said.

'You comfort me.'

'You came here for comfort, I think.'

'Call it that.'

'Will you dine with me tomorrow?'

'With pleasure.'

When she had gone he picked up the telephone. It was an expensive call since transatlantic. He was asked to wait an hour and did so. When the telephone rang back he listened. Nothing was known of Lynne Hammer as agent, but she was a woman with a most interesting ancestry.

THREE

Alidra was an uneasy anachronism. It wasn't formally independent yet, since it still owed some form of feudal duty to a very much larger state to the east of it, but distance and the galloping years had whittled this down to almost nothing. Nevertheless that state still claimed paramountcy, and because it had much more oil than Alidra, because the company which worked that oil was even larger than was Oceanic, no Power was prepared to back a counter-claim. Not that the Old Sheikh had wished to press one. He had paid his annual tribute punctiliously, which had been fixed before the days of oil — ten racing camels, a dish of gold. But the Sheikh was very far from stupid and had realized the disadvantages which this out-of-date arrangement laid on him. Since he wasn't an independent state he had no seat in that curious house in New York which thrived upon the chatter of statelings and their itch to make international mischief; and since his relations with his overlord had been thinned by the years to a thread of legality he couldn't expect that overlord to offer him any effective protection. In any case he was too far away to be useful in any immediate crisis.

But though he saw these disadvantages clearly the Old Sheikh lost no sleep in worrying. Politics he would cope with reluctantly when necessity obliged him to do so, but he wasn't a political animal and his private interests always came first. These were chess and his religion and catamites. Why not, since the future was comfortably secured? It was a pity he had no son himself since from that duty he had drawn back shuddering, but his brother had fathered a perfectly good one, rather a clever boy as it happened, and the Old Sheikh had raised no objection whatever to his brother's proposal for western schooling. It was his instinct that the boy would need it, for he'd recognized that his strange little fief couldn't hope to cheat the years for ever. It was a pity his nephew had begotten no son, but that was a matter of small importance since so far he'd only taken one wife. When the day came for the Old Sheikh to go he'd doubtless take others and be unlikely to fail them. Not from what the Old Sheikh had heard.

So he was a contented old man as he sipped his coffee. A boy on a brocaded cushion was simpering and making advances but the Old Sheikh wasn't feeling amorous. He was feeling like a game of chess and he owed el Hakim a thorough beating. He didn't like Palestinians, none of them, but the doctor was the only man who was anywhere near his class as a player. The others were either no good at all or, if the game by some fluke was getting exciting, they threw it away from a sense of protocol. This annoyed the Old Sheikh to the point of fury. He knew he was held in high regard, but the days had gone when you cut off hands because they'd impiously beaten the Prophet's descendant.

He called a servant and told him to fetch el Hakim. 'And take that tiresome boy away. Give him some money and a couple of clouts. He's as ugly as any woman alive, and why you let him in I can't think.'

On his journey to this strange little stateling, Rifai had had only one fear to nag him, the fear that he might arrive too late. For el Hakim was already there and el Hakim was a man of the gun, a lieutenant of the noisy clown whom Rifai and the Admiral both detested. And he'd only been in Alidra two days when el Hakim paid a call in person. 'Welcome,' he had said. 'You are welcome.'

He had said it with a smile on his mouth but his eyes had been hard with an evident warning. They had said: 'I am the master here. Don't forget it. Do not forget and do not trespass.'

But his tongue had been loud with brotherly greeting. 'Naturally you will join our movement.'

'Naturally,' Rifai said promptly. As things were there was nothing else he could say. But at least his cover was holding strongly. The Israeli Press now called him a terrorist and the exile Arab Press a hero. He had led his men in defence of their land, he'd been captured and had then escaped. If he hadn't he'd have been tortured brutally.

Nobody would suspect such a man of an understanding with an Israeli Admiral.

A week later they gave him a gun. He hid it. He hadn't any use for a gun.

Rifai had found a job quite quickly. Not as good a job as he knew he could do but at least it kept him in modest comfort; it even paid for an ancient car.

He drove in it every week end to the desert, to confirm that his plans were really possible. Alidra, before they'd found oil, had been nothing, a string of villages along the littoral where fishermen wrung a subsistence living from a hot and mostly hostile sea. Now there was a town and the Terminal and hideous concrete barracks for workers. But behind this strip was the bitter desert where the black tents pitched and moved without pattern and the goats were left to ravage whatever grew.

Though el Hakim had got in here before him Rifai hadn't quite abandoned hope, and he drove to this unwelcoming country, looking at it with a prophet's eye. The topsoil was loess, the last stage before sand, but reclaimable with water and care. He knew there had once been water here, and though the water-table had fallen disastrously he believed that the water could still be reached. It would then be a question of men and hard labour. Look what Israelis had done to the Yeshrael. The valley had been a neglected wilderness and the early *kibbutznik* had worked by hand, moving the stones by the sweat of their bodies. Now they had tractors but still they were clearing, cleaning the Croesus soil for two crops a year. Wheat or barley in winter, cotton in summer. Or the Sharon valley a little west, a malarial swamp, tamed and equally fertile.

So here was a tract not for gunmen but husbandmen, a tract which implored you to save and use it. For that he'd accept any help which was offered, even from an Israeli Admiral. He didn't need money, he'd have plenty of that; he needed men who could make a lost land bloom. For that he would pay any price they asked, and they hadn't in fact asked a very high one. What was a little oil against land?

Oil for the skills of reclamation. Good business.

He walked back to his battered car humming softly.

Fair Waved the Golden Corn. . . . He laughed. He had heard his schoolmistress singing it once and had asked her what tune it was. She had told him with some embarrassment since she had married into Islam without reserve. So because she was singing a hymn of her childhood he mustn't suppose she had Christian leanings. Not at all, she was now of the Faith irrevocably. . . . Father, Son and Holy Ghost. More than one God. It was truly shocking.

He drove back to his single room to think, for though the future was unlimited, glorious, the immediate prospects were less than good. For he could see that he'd arrived too late. Another had got in before him and he was precisely the sort of man to murder sense. el Hakim whom they called the doctor, though his profession was no longer medicine. His profession was left wing agitation of exactly the kind which Rifai thought fruitless. He'd had time to build up a faithful following and he meant to take Alidra over. By violence of course, by arms, by shooting. Rifai was sure the attempt would fail, for the Sheikh had a small but efficient army, Yemeni hillmen and formidable fighters. The result of any armed clash was predictable — the disciplined men would defeat the undisciplined as they had in the past and always would; and the attempt would set Rifai back for years. The Old Sheikh was dying, the Young Sheikh summoned, and if he returned to a revolution he'd react as any Ruler would. He would throw out the Palestinians and Rifai would be tarred with a brush he detested. He couldn't go back to his township now and he'd never join men he considered savages.

Wait and pray? Yes of course, but not very hopefully. For he knew that the doctor had smuggled in arms, and arms in the hands of demented men . . . .

He nodded in his chair but woke; he woke to the sound of sporadic gunfire.

It was going to be another massacre. Another Jordan. Another failure.

As he'd said, the food at Russell's club was not as good as once it had been, but they could still put on an acceptable dinner, and the background of candles and smooth male service was perfect for the small business of dalliance. But that wasn't going to be long or tedious. Russell guessed Lynne had made up her mind already. Her approach to the spurious mysteries of sex was masculine in its cool directness; she'd enjoy it if the man attracted her and if it didn't she would find another. Once decided, playing games became tedious, and as for total commitment, whatever that meant, it was a matter for romantic girls. Russell wondered about the late Mr Hammer. He was probably, he decided, a myth.

He woke before she did next morning and made the tea. He found fresh croissants in an airtight tin and he brought her one on a tray with the tea. 'Thank you,' she said sleepily.

'Not at all.'

She sat up in bed and began on the tea, noticing the single croissant. 'Isn't there more than one?'

'There are plenty. But I very seldom eat before lunch.'

'You look like it,' she said approvingly. 'Most of the other men at your club were rather noticeable below

35

the waistline.'

'Most of the other men at my club eat far too much and quite the wrong things.'

'You count calories, then?'

'I do no such thing.' They were as casual as an established couple, cosily relaxed and domestic. Charles Russell, since the subject interested him, began to talk of it with a gentle enthusiasm. 'In the context of the human body calorie is a stupid word. In general it's a measure of energy, specifically of the measure of heat required to raise two pounds of water through two degrees on the Fahrenheit scale. It tells you nothing about the human metabolism. All I do is to watch the carbohydrates.'

'Do you never eat *pasta*?'

'I do — why not? Why deprive myself of something I like? But if I allow myself spaghetti for luncheon I don't eat again for the rest of the day.'

'It's kept you extremely trim and vigorous.'

'It's very kind indeed to say so.' He was sitting on the edge of the bed, wearing an expensive dressing gown which he assumed had belonged to no less than the Prince. 'Could I manage a shave?'

'Of course you could. You'll find shaving gear in the bathroom cupboard. The shower works too.'

'I'm sure it does.'

'What do you mean by that?'

'A compliment.'

He collected his clothes which he'd neatly folded and went away to shave and shower. There were several razors but all of them cutthroats and he hadn't used a cutthroat for years. He nicked himself twice but found cotton wool, and when he had repaired the damage dressed quickly and went back to the living room. Lynne Hammer was already there. She smiled at the dabs of cotton wool.

'I'd forgotten that the Sheikh used a cutthroat. He has a beard and a moustache, you'll remember, but he also has bits where he doesn't grow hair.' She made a half-mocking, half-affectionate gesture. 'Steering round and round his face. He couldn't do that with a modern razor.'

She'd made coffee, bringing a cup to Russell, and he drank it looking round the room. Like its owner's taste in another matter it reflected an almost male practicality. The armchairs were simple but large and comfortable, there was a sofa which was meant to be sat on. A long sideboard generously stocked with bottles and a large and workmanlike desk, very tidy. One wall was entirely hidden by books. There were very few ornaments, no china in cabinets, but two paintings which were discreetly lighted. Russell put them as Flemish revival — not bad. They hadn't the impact of great Dutch masters but they had craftsmanship, and that he respected.

She saw him soaking it up and smiled. 'You like this room?'

'It suits you perfectly.'

'I think I'll keep on this flat when I go abroad.'

He was surprised and didn't trouble to hide it. 'You're going to live abroad?'

'In Israel.'

He didn't answer this but waited.

'You know I'm a Jewess?'

'Not exactly. I know that you have some Jewish blood.'

'How did you know?'

'I checked,' he said.

'You mean you checked me before you took me to bed?' She had risen from her chair but he waved her down.

'Don't be silly, my dear — I'm not a racist. I checked when the Prince first introduced us. I was once in a certain profession, you know, and the relationship was, well, rather interesting. What I checked was your political background and, if it interests you, you have none whatever. But you can't expect that an oil sheikh's mistress won't have files in more than a single office, and what I learnt from one of them was something of your family's history.'

'Political background I may not have, but what about Oceanic Oil?'

'You very wisely told the Sheikh too, and I believe you that he laughed his head off. I think it's a pretty good joke myself. You took money for doing what wasn't necessary and if that isn't a joke I don't know what is.'

'You're a very civilized man indeed.'

'I'm not anti-Semitic, if that's what you mean. On that basis may I ask you a question?'

'I may not answer.'

'I'm going to risk it. Did the Sheikh know about your Jewish grandmother?'

She hesitated before she answered. 'I really don't know — I suspect he did. If *you* checked he had better reason to. But if he did know it didn't matter a damn. It was all too far away, in another world. I don't look like a Jewess, I don't think like a Jewess. In Alidra it would have mattered like hell but I never saw Alidra and never shall. We went most other places and that I enjoyed, but I knew he'd never marry me so I never pestered or put the squeeze on.'

'That's why you were happy.'

'Yes. One reason.' She poured more coffee and smoked a while thoughtfully. 'And now about my Jewish grandmother. My grandfather brought her back from the city and my family didn't take it well. She bore a son and a daughter and my mother's the daughter. She married out too but that doesn't matter. It goes in the female line, as you know. Under Rabbinical law I can claim to be Jewish so I've decided that I'm going to Israel.'

'Your race has very strong roots,' he said.

'You dramatize the whole affair, you make it sound noble and therefore silly. As it happens I'm an American first and you know what we Americans are. We're do-gooders all the way through — we can't help it. So first we make ourselves some money and then we look round for good works to spend it on. The really rich establish Foundations but I'm not in the sort of league to do that. Not that I haven't got quite a bit — the Sheikh gave me a very generous settlement and on top of that there was Oceanic.' She gave him a faintly deprecatory smile. '"Obligation" is a great big word. Better say that perhaps I might be useful. Any visitor — I'll stay American — any visitor with adequate means is very welcome in the state of Israel.'

'A trifle cynical,' he said, 'but true.' He considered before he asked the next question. 'And how are you going to pass your time?'

'I don't know that yet; I haven't thought. Perhaps I could find something useless like one of those unpaid

P.R.Os. who sit in the lobbies of grand hotels explaining to American tourists that everything's okeydoke in Israel.' Her voice changed to a mincing parody. '"The Arabs get the same wages as we do. They even have a vote. They're citizens."' The voice changed back to its normal precision. 'They're citizens, all right. Second class.'

'I don't see you doing a shabby job.'

She said on a sudden note of intensity: 'I don't think you see me at all. Not *me*.'

'I think I do. I see very well. I don't think a lot of your going to Israel but I do understand the whip that drives you.'

'You do?'

'And I respect it.'

'Thank you.'

She rose and poured a third cup of coffee, and when she returned the tenseness had gone. 'Come and see me when you go to Israel.'

'What makes you think I was even considering it?'

'Travel brochures which I saw in your flat — the Canary Islands, Majorca, Israel. Don't go to the Canaries, Charles, they're Blackpool under the sun, quite awful. Parts of Majorca are still very pleasant, but somehow I don't think Majorca's your island.'

'You'll need time to put down roots in Israel.'

'Oh no, I shan't. I've seen an apartment.'

'You've *seen* an apartment?' He was frankly astonished. 'You mean you've been to Israel already?'

'I can guess what you're thinking and the Sheikh didn't know. As I told you, he's a tolerant man, but that would have been a bit too much for him, especially as I was using his money. So one day when he'd gone to New York on some business concerning Oceanic — his uncle left the hard talking to him — I slipped away and had a look.'

'But an apartment,' he said. He'd been doubly astonished.

'You were thinking of a seaside villa, something Italian or maybe Spanish? A garden with parterres and marble urns, a private beach on some charming bay? So was I but I found they don't exist. I looked at Bat Yam and I looked at Herzliyya and I retreated very fast indeed. Both of them are concrete jungles and the coast is as straight as stretched elastic. The Israelis don't go in for villas, or not the sort of villas we mean. The unit of living is the family flat. There are a few old houses but not very many — they've pulled most of them down for blocks of apartments. So a flat it had to be and I've found one, or rather two nice ones knocked into one. It belongs to an American actress, and up to now she's been dithering stupidly. But yesterday she rang up. She'll sell. She thinks there's going to be lots of trouble and she wants to get out while she can. She's chickening.'

'There's going to be more trouble, all right. I'm not an expert on Middle Eastern politics, but Israel can't stand still for long in a state of suspended animation. Either the hawks will go for the jackpot or the Arabs will start another war. A *jihad*, they'll call it. They always do.'

'A war which Israel would win.'

'I think so. And the one after that, maybe, as well. But the sixth or seventh attempt . . .' He shrugged.

'You've answered your own question, Charles. That's why I have to go. I must.'

'Categorical imperative?'

'What?'

'Kant,' he said. 'Never mind. A kraut.'

'You mean a compulsion?'

'A suspect word.'

'You're a strange sort of man as well as charming. Give me a week to clean up the flat.'

'When do you leave yourself?'

'On Wednesday.'

'Ten days will seem a long time without you. I'll go to a hotel to start with.'

'But not for too long.'

'I ardently hope not.'

He went back to his flat and mixed a gin. He didn't often allow a drink so early but he felt he'd earned something stronger than coffee and there were matters he wished to clear his mind on. He'd had sudden affairs with women before, inexplicable if you looked at them coldly, but while they lasted he accepted them gratefully. So Lynne Hammer was not a problem but Israel was.

For on Israel he was wholly ambivalent and ambivalence was a state he detested. On the one hand were his conditioned sympathies and these were pro-Israel without reservation. He hadn't thought of that people as war-like or martial, but there they were, beset and isolated, four times attacked and four times surviving. Five if you counted the War of Attrition. By any normal calculation they shouldn't be on the map at all, but they had fought with something like military genius and always with an unmatched courage. They had earned the right to survive with blood.

On the other side men one could hardly warm to,

and Charles Russell knew enough of politics not to realize that many Arabs felt the same. Not that they dared say so. Never. Palestinians were brother Arabs who demanded support in the name of pan-Arabism. They had often betrayed other Arab hosts but they couldn't themselves be betrayed or negotiated. That was their strength for they had no other. Their military virtues were less than nothing, they had always been whipped with humiliation, not only by the Israeli enemy but by their brethren whom they'd tried too far. And when they did fight they fought from the gutter — the ambush, the hijack, the bomb in the schoolroom.

And yet, and yet, they did have a case. They had lived on their lands for uncounted centuries, mostly under some other state's tutelage, but at least they had lived on those lands securely. And now they had few lands to live on. Citizenship of the state of Israel? But who wanted to be a second class citizen in a culture which was wholly alien?

That was the way the contemporary world thought, especially that part of it paid to say so. To Charles Russell that made the opinion suspect but it didn't yet mean it was falsely founded.

So he'd go back to Israel and make his own mind up. He hated to be left undecided.

Rifai had woken to sporadic gunfire but as he listened it increased and intensified. They'd be running around with their smuggled arms, firing wild bursts at whatever they fancied, but at least they must have a basic plan. They'd go for the central police station first and if they got it they'd start to bargain for terms.

Which Rifai was quite sure that they wouldn't receive. The small but efficient army would crush them. It would bring up its artillery and use it with a casual ruthlessness. Rifai was sick at heart and miserable. That these misguided men, these half-baked Liberators, should be blown to pieces at point blank range was a matter which in no way moved him, but their action would set his own plans back, assuming he survived to try again.

. . . . The police station, yes, and the Palace too. Perhaps he had an outside chance of saving something from the general wreck.

He considered it, suddenly cold and calculating. el Hakim was a dangerous fool in the tradition of an even bigger, but he wasn't by all accounts a coward. The Old Sheikh would have to go, that was evident, and what better Colour to show in false battle than the fact you had done the deed yourself? So el Hakim would not be out on the streets, he'd have gone to the Palace to murder the Sheikh. He had entry any time he fancied. Chess, Rifai thought — he had never been good at it. Nor was he good at killing old men as they sat innocently considering their pieces. But el Hakim would do so without compunction.

Rifai was going to try to stop him. Where that would lead he could not be sure but it would be an act of clear dissociation. That he might turn to his profit.

Might.

He had European clothes and put them on. He found a black bag which resembled a doctor's and into it he slipped the pistol. He had a gentleman's distaste for brawling — that affair with the Israeli Captain had left him with an uneasy trauma — but he was perfectly ready to kill if he had to.

In the street he stopped; he could barely move. This was a quiet, even bourgeois area but now it was as packed as a market. Every accent of the Arab world was shouting in a furious cacophony. Even women were on the streets in force.

He had hoped for a taxi but saw it was hopeless so he began to run in his heavy clothes. Soon he was soaked in sweat; he ran on. In the distance he heard a sound he recognised, the unmistakable bark of a twenty pounder.

Somehow they'd carried the central police station and the army was out and shelling them mercilessly.

At the Palace gates a sentry stopped him; he put a bayonet in his stomach menacingly. Rifai said in English: 'I'm His Highness's doctor.'

The sentry, who spoke no English was puzzled, but he was also rather more than impressed. . . . The heavy European clothes, the sweat, the black bag, the air of urgency. Rifai said in a baby's Arabic, giving it a strong English accent:

'Is there not someone here who speaks English?'

The sentry kept his bayonet pointed but with his other hand he blew his whistle. An officer came out of the guardhouse.

'Can you speak English?'

'Yes. Rather small.'

'I'm His Highness's English doctor from London. He telephoned last night. I have come.'

'Your name, sir?'

'I am Doctor Riffle.'

'I have never heard of a Doctor Riffle.'

'I'm a specialist.'

'What?'

'I treat special diseases.'

The officer nodded: the Old Sheikh had one. But he was a cautious man and he plugged away.

'You say you came here. How did you come?'

'I came by air — there is no other way. I've just landed at the airport.'

'So.' The officer considered it with a Yemeni's unmatched stolidity. So far the story stood up but he had to be sure. 'Why did you not take a taxi?'

'Because there were no taxis there. There was some sort of trouble instead — some firing.'

The officer nodded again: it was true. They had gone for the airport as well as the police station and at the airport they'd been shot to pieces. He looked at Rifai's stained clothes. 'Three miles.'

'I am very tired indeed. I am thirsty.'

The officer sent for water and offered it, and Rifai drank with a word of thanks. The officer was still watching him closely but he was near to making up his mind. He said at length:

'You could have rung for a car.'

'I tried but all the lines were broken.'

It was a guess again but again it was true. The officer's news of events at the airport had come to him by army radio.

'I will take you to His Highness, sir.'

They went up the simple steps of the Palace, through a corridor and up in a lift. It was a very small lift, very old, very stuffy. At the end of another corridor the officer knocked at a double door. A voice said in Arabic: 'Come.'

They went.

The Sheikh had been playing chess with el Hakim. el Hakim had risen to kill with the knife. The Old Sheikh was saying with massive dignity:

'Have the goodness to let me beat you first.'

Rifai put his bag on a table and reached his gun. el Hakim saw him and drew his own. The officer was armed too but did nothing. It was going too fast for a Yemeni hillman.

el Hakim fired first at Rifai and missed. He got the officer who collapsed by numbers. He wasted a precious fraction of time by using a very dirty word, then he tried again for Rifai.

Who'd gone down. The bullet went over his head and broke a vase.

. . . . Typical Liberation shooting.

From the floor Rifai picked him off deliberately. He loathed firearms but had learnt how to use one. el Hakim fell out of his chair in a clumsy heap. The Old Sheikh said calmly:

'Thank you, friend.'

Rifai ran through the corridors down the stairs. He didn't know how to work the lift. He walked past another sentry unchallenged.

Half an hour later they picked him up.

FOUR

The scrappy and always hopeless fighting had almost ended as the Young Sheikh's plane landed but he could see at once that affairs weren't normal. There were armoured cars on each side of the aircraft, keeping station as it taxied in, and when it halted the voice of the pilot came over. There'd been some little local difficulty. Passengers must keep their seats for the moment but His Highness would kindly leave at once as soon as the gangway had been secured.

He went down it to the waiting escort, not the guard of honour he'd often inspected, but grim-faced soldiers in combat order. Their officer saluted creditably.

'The Commander-in-Chief is here, Your Highness. I will take you to his command post at once.'

They drove to what had been called the command post and was normally the V.I.P. lounge. The Commander rose and saluted in turn. 'Welcome, Your Highness. Welcome home.' In the distance there was a burst of fire, suddenly started, as suddenly silenced. The Commander said:

'I'd guess that is the last of them.'

The Young Sheikh didn't waste time in guesses. 'The Palestinians, I suppose.'

'Of course. Those treacherous Palestinian refugees.'

The Young Sheikh looked at the Commander-in-Chief. His rank was in fact Lieutenant Colonel since the Old Sheikh had had no time for Generals, but he was head of a small but deadly army and he was also very much an Arab. So the Young Sheikh said with a due formality:

'Commander-in-Chief, I am properly grateful. The details can come later, I think, but give me the general situation.'

The Commander smiled dourly. 'The usual story. They went off at half cock — they always do. An attempt to seize the media, ill-organized assault on this airport. Hopeless attack on the central police station. All over now.' He shrugged and smiled grimly.

'How many men involved?'

'Say two hundred.'

'Survivors?'

Another shrug. 'Maybe twenty.'

'Where are you holding them?'

'Down in the new stadium, Highness.'

It was the Young Sheikh's turn for a sombre smile. 'There's a precedent for that, a recent one. But don't follow it too closely. No revenge.'

'As Your Highness directs.'

'And my uncle?'

The Yemeni rose and saluted again. He was a punctilious man and not ashamed of it. 'I am sorry to have to report he is dead.'

'Don't tell me they attacked the Palace too.'

'They didn't, or not in a mob like the others. But their leader went there with a knife and a gun. He played a lot of chess with your uncle and they let him in as a regular visitor ten minutes before the fighting started. His name was el Hakim and they called him the Doctor.'

'And he murdered my uncle?'

'Highness, he did not do that.'

The new Sheikh showed a flash of impatience. 'Then tell me what happened.'

The Yemeni told and the Sheikh looked puzzled. 'So my uncle died in his bed hours later?'

'Quite peacefully. He was dying in any case.'

'But why did this second Palestinian, the one you tell me is called Rifai — why did he shoot and kill his leader?'

'If he was his leader. He strongly denies it. Of course with proper interrogation. . . .'

The new Sheikh shook his head at once. 'I don't like that word and that's an order. If a quarter of what you tell me is true this man saved my uncle from death by the knife. God alone knows why but he did so. That is an obligation for ever.' He thought and then asked crisply: 'Where is he?'

'In the stadium with the others.'

'Remove him. Put him in not uncomfortable quarters. There's a file on him?'

'There's a file on every refugee.'

'Then send me Rifai's for my study at leisure. My uncle has been buried?'

'We waited.'

'Rightly. I confirm your action. For the moment there are more urgent matters than inquiry into this strange man's motives.'

These more urgent matters had taken ten days. The Old Sheikh had been quietly but decently buried, for he was a man who had always hated pomp, but the formalities hadn't been only religious. There'd been the men to see whom the Old Sheikh called Ministers, who had assured his successor of total loyalty, and a muster of diplomats of indeterminate status (indeterminate because this stateling's was similar) who had assured him of their consideration. Above all he had felt for the real levers of power. In Alidra there were basically two, the army and the oil which fed it. The Terminal had stopped dead in its tracks, not because the rebellion had sacked it but because the rebels had been largely manning it, and these were now either dead or in custody. But Oceanic had helped the new Sheikh out, flying in engineers and technicians, and the oil was flowing almost normally. He had his hands on the wheel and the rest was with God. He had even had time to read Rifai's file.

A curious story, he thought — most unusual. The Israelis had run the man out as a nuisance, so he'd followed the trail to Alidra and found a job. The Old Sheikh had been properly cautious in granting any form of citizenship, but he'd had an Arab's sense of a host's obligations and exiles from Israel were always well treated. Too well treated the new Sheikh sometimes considered, for look what they had done to other hosts. But the Old Sheikh had felt an imperative duty, so here they were, or rather had been. A handful were left as a sharp embarrassment. The army have been very efficient.

So far the story ran true to form but later it diverged surprisingly. This Rifai was a Palestinian Arab but in Alidra he hadn't mixed much with the others; he had kept to himself in his private life and there wasn't even a hint of evidence that he'd known of the impending coup. On the contrary the evidence strongly suggested that he'd kept away from politics scrupulously, even that he'd been considered aloof.

And on top of that, when the mistimed coup came, he'd gone out and shot its leader dead. The Sheikh sent for coffee and drank it reflectively. Like his uncle he mistrusted Palestinians: they were clannish, untrustworthy, dangerously intelligent. They were the Ibos of the Middle East and look what had happened to Ibos in Africa, what always happened when mere intelligence wasn't backed by more solid and soldierly virtues.

The Sheikh finished his coffee and made up his mind. The story as it stood was nonsense, the essential piece of the jigsaw missing. Iron and fire would doubtless extract it easily, but the Sheikh had a distaste for both, and in any case, whatever his motive, this Rifai had saved the Old Sheikh's life.

He clapped his hands for a servant and sent for Rifai.

Rifai was brought in with a guard whom the Sheikh dismissed. He pointed to a chair. 'Please sit down.' He watched Rifai as he did so silently, then tapped the file on a table beside him.

'I understand you speak English well. I'm not asking out of curiosity — it's a question of what language we use. I've been in the west for quite a time and my Arabic is a trifle rusty.' In fact it was a good deal better than the harsh and oddly accented speech which no Palestinian ever quite lost.

'As Your Highness pleases.' Rifai bowed politely, thinking fast. He was sensitive and extremely quick and he'd realized that he wasn't weaponless. This Sheikh who had power of life and death was also a highly civilized man.

'You are comfortably housed?'

'By your grace and favour.'

'I gather you saved my uncle's life. For that I am under an obligation. As an Arab you will understand me.'

'Your Highness is extremely frank.'

'An inherited privilege. It is also in order to call me "Sir".'

Rifai had decided he'd speed it up. 'So I'm in a comfortable house with a servant but what's left of my misguided countrymen is down in the stadium waiting to die.'

'Those men of yours?'

'They weren't my men.' Rifai spoke with unconcealed contempt. 'I called them misguided — an understatement. I think they were a pack of fools. They had guns in their hands and they misjudged their moment.'

The Sheikh clapped again and ordered coffee for two. Over it, feeling his way, he said:

'What do I do with those few who are left?'

'Entirely your decision, sir.'

'Most are technically Israeli citizens, but you can't expect Israel to take them back.'

'You could try them for treason.'

'And hang them? An outrage! The Press of the world would scream its head off. I haven't solved that problem yet though I can think of a rather neater solution. After all they have abused hospitality and in the old-fashioned Arab world that's a heinous crime.' The Sheikh sat up straight, he was suddenly businesslike; so far he'd been sounding the ground. 'Now tell me why you are here,' he said. 'You weren't in with the Doctor, I quite accept that, so why did you come to this country at all?'

Rifai had made his decision by now. This was a man you could tell the truth to, indeed you must tell the truth or he'd surely outguess you. He said quietly:

'I came to usurp you.'

'My throne? If you call it that.' The Sheikh smiled.

'Not your throne — I would have left you your throne. I came to usurp some land and a little oil. Particularly your barren land. But not with guns like that idiot Doctor. It might have taken a little time but I planned to build a political party, a peaceful one but the real power in the land. I planned to become your Minister. To have your ear and use it to my end.'

'The main end being land to resettle your people?' The Sheikh didn't seem outraged; he said: 'I can see a flaw.'

'I'd be glad to hear it.'

'Once a man has been given a gun he lives by it. The men you were going to bring in would never settle. In any case not all are countrymen. Many are clerks and shopkeepers — townsmen. Put them on any reclaimed land and in no time you'd have a desert again.'

'You are mistaken, Highness.' He'd dropped back to formality. 'I care nothing for the men with guns, they've put themselves outside all comity. But there are plenty of Arabs still in Israel who have never borne arms and never wished to. But nor are they happy as helots in Israel. It was never my intention, never, that armed men should march across your frontier, taking possession of land they couldn't use.'

'I'm glad to hear it,' the Sheikh said drily. He thought for some time. 'But that land of yours — you'd have to reclaim it. The implication was with Israel technicians since you mentioned the little matter of oil and no other people needs oil so badly.' He permitted a smile. 'After you'd got my ear, of course.'

The Sheikh walked to the window and stared down to the courtyard. On the other side of it lived his lawful wife, and soon he would have to take another to bear him the son he both lacked and needed. He said, his back still turned:

'A dream. A noble dream but still a dream.'

'I'm sorry you think so.'

'So am I. But this is Islam, you know, and it always will be.'

'Someday we'll have to move closer to Israel. In watertight compartments, hating each other——'

'I think you're right — I *know* you're right. But I'm certain I haven't the courage to do it.'

'Perhaps when you've sat here a little longer ...'

'My friend, you are a clever man.'

'Not clever, but I am observant.'

The Sheikh would have agreed with 'observant' for he knew that Rifai had been watching him closely, the instinctive and relentless watchfulness which saw everything whilst looking at nothing. And he didn't accept the disclaimer of cleverness. Perhaps wisdom was a better word. This man had much more than the brisk brash intelligence which flawed his race's other gifts .... 'Some day we'll have to move closer to Israel. In watertight compartments, hating each other...'

It was a recipe for stifling stalemate, a passport to yesterday, visa to limbo. This man had had a dream, a vision. A splendid dream but before its time.

'Of course your plan had Israeli connivance.'

'A certain Israeli knew of it. Most did not.'

'A man of the Right, I would guess.'

'As it happened.'

'Would you tell me his name?'

Rifai was silent.

'Perhaps I shouldn't have asked,' the Sheikh said. His manner was as mild as milk but a hint of naked power had surfaced. Rifai noticed it but he wasn't frightened. Maybe he would be soon but not yet.

'So what are you going to do with me?'

'Nothing. You will stay here as my honoured guest. You may not contact your friend in Israel and that I shall have strictly watched. Apart from that you may do much as you please.'

'No conditions?'

'Oh yes, there is a single condition. My uncle was very fond of chess, which led him to make a friend of that Doctor. I don't play chess but I need someone to talk to, so when I send for you you will come and chat with me. In English till I re-master Arabic. Which may not be for a good long time. It's a beautiful language but it isn't elastic.'

Rifai was too wise to offer thanks. 'And what do I do when I'm not your Fool?'

'You might write a book.'

'What sort of book?'

'You wish me to suggest a subject? There is one which has always intrigued me greatly, but I've never possessed the skill to write it and now I do not have the time.' The Sheikh felt for words and finally found them. 'Consider how history might have changed if Christendom had been rather more sensible on the basically simple subject of sex and Islam less absurdly

56

fanatical on the matter of taking a glass of wine.'

The attempted coup in the state of Alidra had had modest but not sensational coverage. Few western papers had given it headlines since the internal affairs of Arab states weren't something which many readers followed, and the conservative Arab papers had played it down. Only the Palestinian Press had blazed it in indignant banners. This was another and shameful betrayal. To Black September must now be added Black June, for the Alidran army had shown small mercy. It was rumoured there were still survivors, a very few survivors indeed, but no names were being given to anyone and the lives of these unhappy patriots were in the hands of a reactionary pig. But fight on brothers, fight on to victory.

There'd been a good deal of this in various keys but the Admiral paid it little attention. He cared nothing for the aspirations of men he considered a theatrical rabble. Rifai had clearly arrived too late, so a carefully matured plan with a chance of success had been destroyed by a man with a gun called el Hakim.

He went into the garden again where the same man was waiting and talking Polish.

'Our channel has gone silent,' he said.

'You think Rifai is dead?'

The other shrugged. 'For his own sake I rather hope he is, and from our point of view it hardly matters. Dead or in prison he still can't operate.'

'He might have gone underground.'

'I doubt it. In a state like Alidra that wouldn't be easy.'

'You must let me think,' the Admiral said.

He went back to his flat and his wife and his breakfast. 'You're looking depressed,' she said.

'I am.'

She didn't answer but served his prodigious breakfast. She had known him for a year by now and for a
woman that was more than enough. She loved him, he
was a very fine man, but his skill in making political
judgements was as limited as his courage was bound-
less. He'd been in politics once but they'd used him,
not listened; they had set him up as a front, the Hero,
whilst they went about the quotidian business of balan-
cing what was politically possible. Which he'd always
been very bad at doing. He was getting on now though
still strong and active, but he was still at heart a fighting man and you'd be foolish to accept his opinions.

She had sensed that he had something brewing and
on the form it would be something questionable. She
was pious as he'd have wished she should be and she
prayed every night that he wouldn't commit them all
Questionable, that was one thing, yes; but foolish
would be quite another. She was his wife and she was
carrying his child.

The Admiral went to his den to think. He wasn't a
sophisticate; he thought with the almost alarming simplicity of the first class commander of men he'd been.
It was understandable that he'd failed in politics, for
there the edges were always blurred and lucidity was
feared and hated. But you didn't win wars by making
compromises; you won them by making the best plan
possible and then steadfastly excluding from it anything that wasn't relevant. Like his now ruined plan to
lay hands on oil. There were Israelis who would have

opposed it bitterly, there were states which would go to the brink of war and one which would almost surely step over it if the enterprise hadn't been settled quickly. Speed had been of the essence. Speed and secrecy.

His wife brought him lime and water with ice and he thanked her with a young man's smile. She liked it when he smiled at her, it reassured her on what she valued most. It wasn't the faintly prurient smile of a man whose wife could have been his daughter but an easy familiar smile to an equal.

When she had gone he went back to thought. Oil had been what he'd always wanted, oil would have been his last gift to his nation. Rifai would have paid for technicians in oil and with oil this dangerously shaky state could laugh in its enemies' faces and go its way.

He stirred in his chair: it might still be done. Geographically it was certainly on since Alidra was less than a hundred miles from the southernmost tip of Israeli territory. There were ships at Eilat and men who still worshipped him.

But he knew that he had powerful enemies, the politicians, the professional compromisers. He despised them, but they still ran the state and their hands were on the state's resources. Those included what was still called Security. It wasn't the world's biggest Service but in efficiency it was one of the best.

It was his hunch that they'd already smelt something. Somebody had said something unwise or somebody had acted suspiciously. Or maybe they had contrived to infiltrate. Their organization was all-pervasive and a man with the Admiral's reputation must

expect an occasional check on his contacts. He ha
always been very careful of those and now he must b
more careful still. He didn't believe he was personall
spied on, but if that happened it would confirm a leak
and a leak would more than double the risk of a
alternative plan which was ripening slowly.

He rose and walked from his cramped little den t
the sun of the even smaller veranda. In the street ou
side was a man doing nothing but he hadn't the air of
casual idler.

The Admiral waited an hour, then looked agai
The first man had gone but another was there still.

So he was under close surveillance at last and the
could only be one explanation of that. His first pla
had leaked and they hadn't liked it. His new one,
they ever discovered it, would put them up like rocke
ing pheasants.

The Admiral made his decision quickly. He coul
telephone to a Minister but he knew the result of an
protest. A polite young man would arrive with
smile. . . . 'Spying on you? My respected Admiral! Ce
tainly there's a man outside, a man on a two-hou
watch — it's that serious. But of course he isn't a sp
he's a guard.'

And it wouldn't be unreasonable, the Admir
couldn't prove the opposite. He was a prime target f
Palestinian terrorists, indeed there had been tw
attempts already.

So it was pointless to telephone — there the ma
was. He thought again of speed and secrecy. Bo
might still perhaps be relevant.

He must contact Ben Arie and do it at once. Be
Arie knew the contemporary ropes, Ben Arie was

man he trusted.

And Ben Arie was the Admiral's Judas. The men outside would report his moves but Ben Arie had betrayed him already.

FIVE

Lynne Hammer was being seen off by Charles Russell.
'I'm excited,' she said.

'I can well believe it. A brand new life——'

'It's not only that. I've just done a very unwomanly thing, bought a flat which I've only seen twice in my life. A hunch if there ever was one, Charles.'

'I only hope it turns out as you want it.'

'So do I. But you're coming to see for yourself.'

'Since you ask me I most certainly am. But I'd like to be the tourist too and stay at a hotel to start with. I might go up to Jerusalem too. I've a friend who has retired thereabouts. We don't write much but we send regular cards.'

'Then give me a week to fix the apartment.'

'I will but it's going to seem a long one.'

He saw her up to Departure politely, then went back into the bar for a drink. He ordered gin and tonic unhesitatingly. Sherry, in any airport on earth, wasn't something he was prepared to risk. At the bar was an Inspector of Police whom he'd once known rather better than most. There'd been nothing secret about their professional relationship and no reason in the world to conceal it. Charles Russell said:

'Good morning, Inspector. What are you drinking?'

'The same as you, please.'

'Travelling?'

'No, I work here. Security.'

'Interesting?'

'Sometimes very. Mostly it's a routine slog but every now and then there's a crisis. Take last week, for example.'

'All right, take last week.'

The ex-Inspector took a drink and sighed. 'So this charter flight comes in from Israel full of delegates to some Jewish conference. It lands normally, and then the hoo-hah. For what do you think the pilot wants?'

'I haven't an idea. You tell me.'

'He wants fuel to fly straight back to Israel.'

'Without landing his passengers?'

'Not a one. Not even two stiffs and a brace of wounded.'

'You're telling me he'd been hijacked?'

'No. I'm telling you he *hadn't* been hijacked. There'd been an attempt right enough but they'd fought it off. Israel is pretty tough about hijacks.'

'So I have heard.'

'You have heard correctly. They have guards and the guards are armed. It's unpopular with other air lines.'

'And other things than guards,' Russell said.

'You've heard that too? It's more than possible.'

'But what sort of things? I haven't heard that.'

'Your guess is as good as mine, but *things*. Things that go bump and bang and puff. Things that knock you down when you're looking elsewhere.' The Inspector smiled a professional smile. '"This animal is very wicked. When attacked it has been known to defend itself." But it wasn't like that in the business last week — just an old-fashioned gun battle which the Israeli guard won. He got wounded and so did a panicky passenger, but two Algerians were very dead indeed.'

'An embarrassing cargo to land with.'

'Quite. And a good deal worse than that for us. Th
top brass got on the blower to London and the rest o
us talked to the pilot by radio. The idea was to hol
him quiet a bit while the big boys decided and gave u
orders. And what he told us made it a good deal worse
or some people seemed to think it did. The shoot-u
hadn't occurred in our airspace, but I couldn't see tha
made much difference. The last thing H.M.G. woul
want would be a couple of Algerian stiffs and som
story of Libyan money behind them.'

'So what happened then?'

'It happened fast. A man came tearing out fror
their embassy. Pretty brusque, he was, but he needn'
have been so. The Home Office had beaten him to it
We were to give the pilot fuel and clearance. And fo
God's sake don't waste time about doing it.'

'So the story never made the papers.'

'The incident never made the papers because no jour
nalist got within smell of a story. And when that plane
load got back to Israel I reckon they kept their face
buttoned. I'd guess Israel has pretty efficient machir
ery for persuading people to keep their traps shut.'

'You have an interesting life,' Charles Russell said

'It can be sometimes — it's mostly routine.' The ex
policeman ordered drinks in turn. 'Checking passer
gers as they go through Departure. I know it all looks
bit amateurish, but you can take it that what you se
isn't everything. We're as efficient as any airport o
earth but there are problems which we'll never solve.

'Such problems as?'

'They're always changing things about — the actua

layout of the Terminal proper and the routes different types of traffic use. Ambulances are a particular nuisance. And there are always those conceited diplomats. You know what they are — all rights and privileges. Lay a hand on them and they'll scream to the Foreign Office.'

'I always thought that was much overdone.'

'You can say that again — it certainly is. We slip them through a beam of course, but there are several sorts of weapon a beam won't show.'

'Has a diplomat ever been caught with a gun?'

'Not so far, sir. Or not at Heathrow.'

'You've been lucky,' Charles Russell said.

'Precisely. But in Security you can't play luck.'

'You're telling me.'

'I beg your pardon. And there's something else besides luck, alas. What keeps me awake at night is the big one.'

'The big one?'

'That's what I said — the coup, the big one. You think of everything that's humanly possible and then you do your damnedest to block it. Then some murderer pulls the mat out under you. I don't like any sort of terrorist but there's no denying they're smart as monkeys. So one of them dreams up something new, something you've had no reason to think of, and there you're with the can tied firmly, losing your job as likely as not, and with two hundred lives on your conscience for ever.'

'You think that could happen?'

'I *know* it could happen.' The ex-Inspector finished his drink. 'If I prayed I'd ask you to pray for us too.'

Charles Russell opened the door that evening on a stout young man who was standing outside it. 'I've been sent all the way from Israel to see you. I work for a certain organization.'

'Can you prove it?'

'No.'

'Then you probably do.' Charles Russell knew the form from experience. If this large young man had produced an authority Russell would have slammed the door in his face, for if he was what he claimed to be anything like an identification would be the last thing he'd keep on his formidable person. Russell hesitated — he'd been jumped more than once — but finally he said: 'Come in.' He put the stranger in a chair and waited.

The young man smiled. 'My name's Joe Beholden and I know what you're thinking. From my age I must have been born in Israel, but I'm not a sabra, I was born in East London.'

Charles Russell's face didn't move a muscle though he'd picked up the unmistakable accent. It was also a reassuring accent because hard to acquire if you hadn't been born to it. This Beholden was probably telling the truth. Charles Russell said:

'But you went to Israel?'

'I went when I was sixteen — I'm now thirty. It hit me one day. I had to do it.'

'Your race has very strong roots,' Russell said. He had said it to Lynne Hammer before and Lynne Hammer had slid away from it shyly. But Beholden took it without a blink.

'So now I work for the people you mentioned. Or rather the people you didn't mention since you were tactful enough not to force me to name them. Your Executive once had fraternal relations so I've been sent here to ask you a simple favour.'

'I'm retired and I haven't the power to help you.'

'Not a positive favour — something quite negative. We'd rather you didn't visit Israel.'

'How do you know I'm going to Israel?'

'That's as easy as it possibly could be. We get lists from our air line as a matter of course. Anything like a V.I.P. and we start to take a professional interest.'

'I see,' Charles Russell said; he thought. 'And why shouldn't I go to Israel, please?'

'Because you're still Charles Russell.'

'Nonsense. I'm a retired official like any other.'

'That isn't our view and I'm here to state it. You'd be a prize as a hostage and our policy's final. We never bargain over a snatch or a hijacking — no release of criminals, no money, no nothing. In the unlikely event that they snatched our President we would write him off like anyone else. I'm convinced that's the only way to handle them and if others would do the same that would end it. But I have to confess there's a disadvantage. The tougher you get with plain extortion the more they move towards mindless violence — sabotage, bombings, murdering babies. By splinter groups all disowned publicly but privately financed from one source. I don't pretend to admire such people.'

'But I thought you tried to encourage tourism.'

'We do when it shows a profit. You wouldn't. We'd feel we ought to put a guard on you and we've enough on our hands without doing that.'

'I wasn't asking for any such thing.'

'I know. And even if we did put a guard on we don't

pretend to infallibility. There's such a thing as straight bad luck. You don't have to be a Zionist, which as far as I know you never were, you don't have to look at an Arab sideways, to be sitting in a café drinking and a grenade comes from nowhere and kills or maims you.'

Charles Russell said quietly: 'You need a drink.' Fatah had threatened all tourists as enemies: anyone who brought profit to Israel was an enemy of its much publicized cause; anyone who brought profit to Israel had only himself to blame if he died.

'That's very kind indeed. I do.'

Russell mixed them and Beholden drank. 'Then if I can't persuade you to stay in England I can only ask for cooperation.'

'What sort of cooperation?'

'Practical. The air line told us you'd bought a ticket and you'd been to our Tourist Agency first. We know where you're going to lodge but your movements . . .?'

'I'm staying at that hotel to start with, then I'm moving in with a friend indefinitely.'

'May I ask your friend's name?'

'It is Mrs Lynne Hammer.'

'We know something of a Mrs Lynne Hammer.'

Charles Russell said with a crisp annoyance: 'For a woman who's only arriving this evening you seem to be very well informed.'

Joe Beholden hadn't taken offence. 'She was an oil sheikh's mistress once, you know.'

'But that oil sheikh isn't anti-Israel. If you had such a thing as a friend in the Arab world——'

'He's certainly much less bitter than many. But she also reported to Oceanic.'

'Taking them for a ride in the process.'

Joe Beholden nodded appreciation. 'You seem to be well informed yourself.'

'I told you I was going to stay with her.'

'Mrs Hammer is very welcome indeed — any visitor who can pay his way is always very welcome indeed. I'm afraid it's you who isn't welcome.'

'Back to that again?'

'Well, who else do you know?'

He's a sticker, Charles Russell thought — a good one. Of course he was, they were all of them competent. 'I know a man who's called the Admiral.'

Joe Beholden suddenly sat up straight. '*The* Admiral?'

'There are more than one?'

'There's only one called so.' Beholden hesitated, assessing Russell. If he offended him he'd get no further, but equally if he beat about he would irritate with the same result. He said at last with his first uncertainty:

'I suppose there's a story somewhere.'

'Of course. And I don't see why I shouldn't tell you.' Charles Russell was rather liking Beholden, his mixture of professional skill and a wholly natural ear for the truth. He was offering Russell several options but none of them was brass faced lying. 'So more years ago than I care to remember I was serving with my regiment in London. I got very bored with London service — mounting the Guard and all the rest of it — and at the time there was only one war to go to. So I asked for a secondment and got it. In fact I got rather more than I'd asked for.'

'In what was then Palestine?'

'Yes indeed.'

'It was there you met the Admiral?'

'Hm. He wasn't an admiral' then but a sergeant. Except that he was in Irgun Zvai Leumi and they didn't go flashing three stripes on their jackets. So I went out with a patrol one night and they ambushed us very neatly indeed. Somebody put a noose round my neck. I'd never been quite so frightened before. Then a man comes out of the night from nowhere and starts bawling the others out in dog German. I happen to understand dog German and he was telling them they were a disgrace to their cause. He told me he had no use for prisoners and he didn't hang men in cold blood like an animal. So he took off the noose and he kicked me out. Literally. He put his boot in my arse.'

'And you're friendly still?'

'Why ever not? Later we picked him up ourselves and I was a member of the Court which tried him. I was only a junior officer then, and when I threw my own small weight about it was very much disapproved of and rightly. But in the end he got two years, no more.'

'Irrelevant since he escaped after one.'

'Not irrelevant since he might have got ten. Not irrelevant to what's now the Admiral.'

'An interesting story.'

'Not very. There are tales about the Troubles which stink but there are also tales which are not discreditable. Your Admiral is a man of integrity. I hope that doesn't sound pompous.'

'No.'

Russell saw that Beholden's glass was empty; he refilled it and waited. Beholden asked:

'How well do you still know our famous Admiral?'

'I don't really know him at all — we're contacts. I send him a card at Rosh Hashana and he sends me others at Christmas or Easter. I haven't seen him since then but I certainly mean to.'

'We'd much rather you didn't.'

'So I had gathered. But give me a good reason not to.'

Joe Beholden didn't answer directly. 'We take orders from the party in power. As you did, sir.'

'That's correct. More or less. I don't say we didn't bend them sometimes.'

'Perfectly understandable — so do we. But not towards the Admiral.'

'No? Then what does this old Admiral want?'

'Why need I name it to Colonel Russell since I can't prevent an intelligent guess? He wants what alone would make us viable, pay our debts and give us real independence.'

Charles Russell was silent; he knew something of oil. Oil had disappointed Israel. Geologists had assured it was there and geologists had been consistently wrong. Joe Beholden shortly broke his thoughts.

'We got hold of a bit when we whipped the Egyptians but the Americans made us give it up. I'm not the Admiral's man — he's too dangerous — but I share his mistrust of American policy. There's a large Jewish vote, they send money and arms, but when we win prizes they take them away.'

'The Admiral can't be wild enough to be thinking about Sinai again. It would mean going back to the Suez Canal.'

'There is oil in other Arab states and some of them are pretty weak. You wouldn't need a regiment of soldiers, just a handful of determined men.'

'*To send up half the world in flames.*'

'And the Admiral isn't alone or I wouldn't be here. There are several others who think as he does.'

'You're suggesting he's a little ga-ga?'

'He's a very long way indeed from ga-ga. What he suffers from is Hero's Disease.'

'What the devil's that?'

'It's a sort of time-lag. The clock stopped at your finest hour. Time has washed you up on a beach and left you, but you still have men who would follow you blindly.'

'I'm not intending to join them, you know.'

'I didn't suppose you were.'

'And so? I told you I'd be a simple tourist.'

Again Beholden answered obliquely. 'As you'll have noticed from the English newspapers we're tending to move Right rather sharply. But not to the dotty Right. Not yet. Nobody wants another war.'

'Only the fruits of war,' Russell said.

'That's what the cynics say — I'm not one of them. I believe we're entitled to use what we hold from past wars which were all of them brutally forced on us. To bargain with it for solid peace, maybe to keep enough space to defend ourselves. But the Admiral would go further than that. You know he fought with Irgun Zvai Leumi. Do you remember its battle song?'

'No.'

Beholden began to hum a tune. Russell had never known the words but he knew the title: *Both Sides of the Jordan.* And he remembered the secret army's emblem, a clenched fist with a suitably menacing rifle. There was little to that, it was a military cliché, but the background to the clenched fist and the rifle had been a map of the whole of Mandatory Palestine. And that had included the state of Jordan.

'He can't be as crazy as that,' Russell said.

'You're thinking of Jordan? No, he doesn't want that. No Israeli wants the whole of Jordan. There's no oil there and we don't need more deserts.'

'Interesting. No doubt you're right. But none of this touches a simple tourist.'

'You are also Charles Russell — you'll never escape it.' Joe Beholden finished his drink and rose. 'I can't change your mind?'

'I'm afraid you can't. I'll be a tourist as I said and behave like one. My conduct will be quite impeccable.'

'It isn't *your* conduct, Colonel Russell, which has my Minister biting his nails. In daily life one plays the percentages but in Security one doesn't dare to.'

'The chances that any tourist gets hurt must be thousands to one and probably more.'

'I accept those figures.'

'Then why are you fussing?'

'Because you're not an ordinary tourist.'

'We've been through all that before.'

'We have not.' For the second time Beholden hesitated. 'You want it straight?'

'I prefer it straight.'

'You're accident-prone,' Beholden said. 'If there's anything going it comes your way. Look at the last few years of your life.' He walked to the door. 'Think it over, Colonel.' He shut the door behind him quietly.

Charles Russell sat on in astonished silence. He'd never thought of it that way but perhaps it was true. Joe Beholden had thrown a sucker-punch but it had landed with uncomfortable accuracy.

The three of them sat in a comfortable flat for they had almost unlimited money behind them. They were what Beholden had called a splinter group and they were dedicated to the destruction of Israel. But in pursuing this disagreeable end they saw no reason to live disagreeably. The woman had been born in England but had spent time in a West German prison. One man was Irish, the other an Arab, though in the European clothes he was wearing he would have passed as a southern European.

In the background a record player thumped noisily. It was the Top of the Pops of the moment — *Pull it Down*. The whining, self-pitying voices droned on, affecting mid-Atlantic accents, reaching for the ultimate jackpot, the American tour which they'd never make. . . . Pull it Down, Pull it Down, Pull the Old Men Down. It was more than a successful Pop, it was the anthem of a sub-culture collapsing. The men were lapping it up ecstatically, it released their own furious futile repressions, but the woman thought it bourgeois and pointless. She said to the Arab:

'Turn that off.'

He allowed a frown but obeyed the order. The Irishman said:

'This is a gift from God.'

The woman scowled for she didn't like it. She was a dialectical materialist and any mention of God offended her prejudices. She wore spectacles and a fringe of black hair and she looked like a wayout progressive schoolmarm. In fact she'd been thoroughly trained and indoctrinated and had killed in the coldest blood more than once. The two men accepted her leadership since they must. The woman began to tick if off, to make sure that the two male pigs understood her.

'So this First Secretary in the Israeli embassy goes and blows himself up on some patent stove. His face is very severely damaged and he's going to need first class plastic surgery. He could get that in England as well as anywhere but he wants to have his family round him. He would.' Her already contemptuous face became more so. 'You know what Israelis are about families.'

'Naturally,' the Arab said.

'So they arrange to fly him home for surgery and they do it in a tearing hurry — ambulance to the airport tomorrow. All the arrangements are here in detail.' She tapped a paper on the table before her. 'I can't tell you where the tip-off came from — there's a block between us and the friend who gave it — but my instructions are that this friend is reliable and the essential is very simple indeed. You can't carry a stretcher through normal Departure so this ambulance will have ambulance clearance all the way through to the tarmac where they'll load. That's a bit unusual but not outrageous, for how could an Israeli diplomat endanger an Israeli aircraft? and doctors and nurses and medical orderlies aren't normally thought of as risks to security. That is, if anyone's thought at all. It's more likely that since this man is a diplomat everyone will be leaning backwards. V.I.P. slop for V.I.P.s. So in the ambulance will be this Israeli First Secretary, plus a doctor and nurse and an orderly-driver.' She looked at the others. 'Now take it from there.'

The Irishman asked: 'We snatch the ambulance?'

'Obviously we snatch the ambulance.'

The Arab said in his stolid way: 'One or two questions.'

'Ask them by all means.' The Arab bored the woman stiff but he had the sort of mind which saw dangerous holes.

'We'll have to make the snatch quite early, not anywhere near the actual loading point.'

'Perfectly correct again.' The woman produced an aerial photograph which had been taken from a Libyan aircraft: 'That's the general layout up at Heathrow.' She pointed with a pencil. 'There. Ambulances go in at that gate.'

'You're sure of it?'

'I did the fieldwork while you two were asleep. I was obliged to check since they've an itch for changing things.' She was cool and she was wholly confident. The others didn't like her bossiness but accepted what she said as correct.

She pointed with the pencil again. 'There — a ring road. There's a certain amount of sporadic traffic so we'll have to work fast — get it right first time.'

'The details?' the Arab asked.

'Are these.' She began to recapitulate quietly. 'First overtake the ambulance and block it with the least fuss possible.' She nodded towards the Irishman briskly. 'Then you take the driver and don't do it noisily. He'll probably be middle aged and ambulance drivers don't carry guns. Then join us two at the back and we all get in. It's very unlikely the doors will be locked but if they are I've a toy to deal with them. If the doctor has a white coat Patrick takes it and I shall want the nurse's

uniform. After that we'll have no further use for them.'
She was entirely matter-of-fact and casual. 'The doctor may well be Jewish anyway.'

'The dead driver will still be in front.'

'Oh no. There's a door between his cab and the rest of it so the attendant can get inside directly when he changes from driving to helping with stretchers. We open it and pull in the body. Hani here takes his uniform and goes back through the door to drive on in his place.' She turned to the Arab again emphatically. 'And make sure of which pocket he keeps his pass in. There's certain to be a check at some point but in the circumstances it's going to be formal.'

'We'll have to work fast.'

'Very fast indeed.'

'And the man on the stretcher?'

The woman stared. 'Naturally we take him with us — he's our passport to getting on to the aircraft. Fine fools we'd look with an empty stretcher.'

'Suppose he gives the alarm as we do it?'

'If he isn't already sedated I'll see to it. What's important is that he's our principal target. Those Israelis boast that they never negotiate but no one has yet snatched one of their agents. For that's what he is as it happens — an agent. The diplomat business is just his cover and he's a pretty big man in the set-up he works for. The Israelis may claim they never parley, and for ordinary hostages, yes, that's true. But they simply can't risk that this man would talk; he could blow their whole network sky high in ten minutes. And they'll know that we could make him talk. A sick man could hardly hold out for long however well trained and however brave. So they'll give us what we want, our comrades, and they'll do it without fuss or delay.'

The Irishman said again: 'It's from God.'

The woman would have admitted some luck but any mention of God was too much.

'Shut up.'

SIX

Charles Russell wasn't always impressed by Security at major airports, and despite what the ex-Inspector had told him he didn't rate Heathrow higher than adequate. For any ordinary journey, that is. But for Israel it was another matter, much tighter to the point of severity. There'd been no question of checking his bags in locked, leaving them to whatever inspection might be taking place behind the scenes: instead he took them through a clearly-marked channel where he opened and saw them searched by hand. Then another bench for cabin luggage before passing the electronic detector. Beyond it was a polite young man who spoke English but very possibly wasn't and who frisked him with a professional competence. Russell had been frisked more than once and he knew that on more than one occasion he could have hidden a gun if he'd seriously wished to. But never from this smiling young man. He knew his job and was taking it seriously. Finally in the aircraft itself there was a careful and equally thorough body count.

Russell was a provident man and was staying at a hotel to start with so he was travelling on a package ticket. In any case there was no First to tempt him since the whole aircraft had been stripped to Tourist, giving twelve extra seats where the First Class had been and a clear view up the central aisle to the door beyond which sat the Captain and crew. The aircraft was a little old fashioned, evidently not the Queen of this airline, but she was a type which Russell had often flown in and he knew which seat to make for and got it. On the starboard side just behind an escape door. There wasn't another seat in front of it, you could put down your bag in comfort and stretch your legs, and a pantry was just opposite, offering the chance of an early drink if you were agreeable to the stewardess working it. Russell could be extremely agreeable when he needed a drink before a meal.

He looked around with a keen curiosity, reflecting that the ex-Inspector had spoken with a certain hyperbole. 'Things that go bump and bang and puff. Things that knock you down when you're looking elsewhere.' Almost certainly that was exaggeration but equally there'd be several precautions which other airlines would consider unnecessary. Cameras probably, carefully hidden, feeding a screen on a desk in the flight cabin, and of course they'd be able to seal that cabin. When the policy was Never Negotiate the pilot, whatever happened behind him, must be free to fly home to the final scene, the last and possibly tragic act which that policy risked and accepted deliberately.

And of course there'd be at least one guard. Charles Russell looked around again. There were several Rabbis sitting together, reading books which he assumed were devotional, but another was sitting apart and alone, reading *The Financial Times*. He had come aboard just ahead of Russell and Russell had noticed the way he moved. Rabbis had a special walk, as Catholic priests had a special walk, but this man had moved with an athlete's ease, climbing the steps of the gangway briskly. He was dressed in the orthodox black and wore a beard but there was something about that beard . . . . Russell wondered. A trifle too luxuriant for a man who was young still and obviously active? A faint hint of the Green Room? Yes, perhaps. So if anyone had offered a bet as to who on this aircraft was armed and wary Russell's money would have gone on this Rabbi.

A stewardess passed him and Russell hailed her. 'When we get off the ground I'd love a drink.'

'I'll make it my business to see you get one.'

She gave him a frank and friendly smile, a fraction warmer than her duty demanded. She liked the look of this middle-aged man and his manner. He neither begged nor demanded but stated a need, accustomed to those needs being met. Too many passengers grovelled or bullied and the stewardess had grown bored with both. Russell for his part liked the look of the stewardess. From her age she must have been born in Israel and he reflected, as had many before him, how astonishingly a race could change when it was walking on its own soil in freedom. If you looked rather hard this young woman was Jewish but also she was something else; she was a handsome Mediterranean female. She might have been Neapolitan and Russell suspected her parents still were. Later he'd try her and check his guess. His Italian was still rather better than good.

'I'll bring you a drink just as soon as we're flying. You know what the rules are.' She raised a shoulder. 'Silly, but we don't dare break them. And I'm afraid there may be a bit of delay. The Captain's just going to tell you why.'

They had halted on a tarmac apron, a little short of the final runway and takeoff, and the Captain's voice came over the speakers. He spoke in Hebrew first, but briefly, much happier in the English which followed.

'I'm sorry that there's a little delay but we're going to pick up an urgent stretcher case. If you will bear with us it shouldn't be long.'

From the starboard side where he sat in some comfort Charles Russell could see the ambulance halting. A nurse got out first, then two men with a stretcher. One wore a doctor's long white smock, the other an attendant's uniform. Russell, who still had a soldier's eye, noticed that it fitted badly and moreover bore a row of ribbons which its wearer was too young to have earned. He shrugged — such things happened. Some elderly man became suddenly sick and somebody else, not on outside duty, took his uniform since he now had to have one. The nurse shut the doors of the ambulance quickly and the procession moved out of Russell's sight to the motorized ramp which had followed the ambulance and been raised to the forward door to receive it.

He saw them again as they brought in the stretcher. One of the crew stood ready to help them, and from the stripes on his sleeve he must be the Third Officer. Charles Russell had flown on this aircraft before and he knew that it didn't need a Third Officer. So doubtless he would have other duties. Perfectly natural, indeed reassuring. They slid the stretcher across three vacant seats where the armrests had been removed beforehand and the Third Officer shut the open door. The nurse and the doctor and male attendant sat down on three seats just in front of the stretcher. The Third

Officer asked them:

'Okay?'

'Okay.'

He went back into the flight deck's sanctuary, closing that door in turn behind him. Russell could see the ramp move away but the ambulance stayed where it was on the apron. Again there was the voice of the Captain.

'I apologize but we still have clearance.'

He had stopped his engines but now restarted them. He began to taxi slowly forward, then positioned himself on the runway meticulously. A moment's delay, then he revved for takeoff. Twenty-five seconds later they were flying. To Russell who knew the statistics of flight they had always been twenty-five very long seconds.

The No Smoking and Fasten Seat Belts signs were still alight as the stewardess came to him. There was an empty seat on his left hand side and she let down the flap and put his drinks on it. There were two miniatures of gin and one tonic.

'Two?' Russell asked.

'I guessed you could use them. And I'll bring you your lunch in about an hour.'

'Do me another kindness — forget it.' Like many men who travelled on aircraft he only ate on them if hunger obliged it and this flight was a mere four hours. Why risk it? 'I think I'll take a nap.'

'Happy dreams.'

He finished his morning ration of drink and five minutes later was fast asleep. He had the gift of instant sleep and had needed it.

In the airport's Control Room they'd called the chief to give orders since the ambulance was still on the apron and they'd failed to raise the driver by radio. The chief was looking through binoculars and the ex-Inspector was standing beside him. There were airport policemen outside the Control Room but since a recent and never publicized incident a Security man must be present inside it and it was the ex-Inspector's turn for this duty. The chief was barely keeping his temper.

'That driver must be drunk or have had a stroke. In any case we must move him at once.' He was a very angry man indeed but his orders were cool and comprehensive; he turned to the ex-Inspector beside him. 'Harry. Take a patrol car and the duty doctor. Never mind the police just now — they can do their stuff when we find out what's happened. For the moment the priority is to get that thing away from there before there's anything like a major disaster.'

The ex-Inspector found the doctor quickly and they drove quicker to the offending ambulance. They looked in the driver's seat. There was no one.

'Odd,' the ex-Inspector said. The doctor said nothing, it wasn't his business.

'We'd better open up the back.'

They did so and for a second froze. Three bodies were strewn on the floor, unmoving. One man was still in his shirt and trousers but a woman and another man had been stripped till they wore only their underclothes. As they stared the woman whimpered and opened her eyes.

The sound dissolved their shock into action. The doctor gave only a glance at the men but went to the woman and knelt beside her. The ex-Inspector looked at the men but he didn't need to kneel to know. One had died by the knife and the other been battered. From what was left of his face he might once have been Jewish.

. . . . Savagery. Insensate savagery.

The doctor closed his bag and rose. 'The woman may live if we can get her in fast enough. Use your blower to call the station ambulance.'

The ex-Inspector did so and waited, but the doctor said:

'I'll stay here. You report.'

There was a brief exchange on the patrol car's radio and the doctor heard an immediate order. 'Come back and give me the details at once.'

The ex-Inspector drove away. The Big One, he was thinking again. This time it was the really Big One.

In the Control Room the chief was writing a message. The flight to Tel Aviv was in danger. One man would be dressed to look like a doctor, a second was wearing an ambulance uniform. There was also a woman who'd look like a nurse.

It was succinct and urgent and gave the known facts. Speculation was for the moment pointless. The chief passed the message across his desk.

'Send that to the pilot and keep on sending it. Keep on sending it till you get acknowledgement.'

SEVEN

Russell's surmise had been perfectly right: the Third Officer had indeed special duties. He ran anything electrical, and in this aircraft there was apparatus which the aircraft of other lines didn't carry. At this moment he was listening hard, taking the message which came from Heathrow. He wrote it down and checked by repeat; he wanted to be sure beyond question. Then he took the Captain the paper silently.

The Captain read it without change of expression. He had served in the Israeli air force and had a row of medals to prove his competence, but there were other things than competence: there were the rules. Sensible rules distilled experience and one of them was unbendingly mandatory. The Captain stayed in command of his aircraft — in proper command, never flying at gunpoint. No flying around the Med under durance, seeking one haven and then another. If some hijacker started to murder passengers, if some hijacker cracked and blew the tail off, that would never be held against a Captain. What would lose him his job and maybe worse would be to land at some Arab airport tamely because an Arab was holding a gun to his head. He said to his Third:

'Lock the door at once.'

The Third Officer did so and returned to the Captain. 'What do I do now?'

'Acknowledge as asked and let me think.'

And indeed the Captain had need to do so. So far his orders had come on a reflex but now he was in a real uncertainty. For the rules were based on past experience and experience itself on precedent. The Captain thought hard but couldn't remember one. He knew no precedent for a Captain, in flight, being warned from the ground that he carried hijackers, even who those hijackers were. For once he would have to play it by ear and he very much preferred the rule book.

Send his Third back to shoot it out? He would go. Reuben also carried a gun but two against three wasn't tempting odds, and in any case shooting it out was dangerous. If passengers got killed or injured he'd be blamed for an unnecessary gunfight. But he had other resources and decided to use them. He said to the Third again:

'See if the box helps.'

The Third Officer went back to his desk, fiddling with dials and switches. He had four cameras and the third brought it in. The picture rolled for a moment and then steadied clearly.

'The nurse and the doctor are by the stretcher. The doctor is using a hypodermic. The attendant is still sitting smoking.'

'No sign of weapons?'

'None I can see.'

'Has the doctor a bag?'

'He has.'

'I feared so.'

The Captain thought it over deliberately. 'Warn Reuben at once — you know how to do it. And get Ruth on the pantry blower discreetly. She's much the steadiest and won't give it away. Before they show their hands, I mean. The other two girls had better not know.'

The Third Officer found a red button and pressed it and the Rabbi got the message at once. He got it from the seat below him. There was no audible sound, just a quick vibration. It ticked his bottom but only once. That meant Alert but Take No Action. In the pantry the stewardess answered the telephone.

'I think you'd better look yourself, sir.'

The Captain gave the Second the aircraft, then came over and looked at the screen without comment. He didn't need to comment now; he'd been in doubt before, there had been no precedent. But now there was a rule and a clear one. The uniformed man was coming closer. Suddenly he went off the screen and the Third began to fiddle his instruments. The Captain said:

'It doesn't matter. The door is locked as I said?'

The Third Officer nodded.

There was the sound of a pistol butt rapping peremptorily.

'Activate,' the Captain said.

The Third Officer pulled a switch. 'She's on.'

The elderly lady from Golders Green had not believed what her sharp eyes had seen. The man in an attendant's uniform had rapped and put his hand on the door handle. Then his back had arched like a bow and he'd fallen. Now he was slumped against the door.

The Third had him now on another camera, the Captain looking over his shoulder. The Captain said:

'Turn it off.'

The Third did so.

The lady from Golders Green screamed hysterically. Her painted mouth stayed open, dribbling.

The Captain said thoughtfully: 'Three little nigger boys.'

'I beg your pardon?'

'A rhyme for children. The important thing is that now there are two.'

They'd served luncheon without waking Russell but when you woke from sleep at a woman's scream your faculties returned very promptly. He took in the situation quickly, assessing the position tactically. Of the two who were facing down the aircraft the doctor held an automatic and the nurse had one grenade in her hand and another at a belt round her waist. A third man had inexplicably fallen but the reason for that could wait till later. Russell looked at the Rabbi he'd guessed was armed but he hadn't a field of fire without rising and if he did so the doctor would get him first. Assuming he knew his business.

Which one must.

He noticed that the seat beside him was now occupied by the senior stewardess. He raised an eyebrow: she nodded briefly. 'The other two girls are in seats behind us. There's a drill for this and we know what to do.'

The cabin was utterly silent, suspended.

Charles Russell's first feeling was one of relief. The nurse might have shouted that this was a hijack and the cliché would have rasped his nerves rather more than the prospect of imminent danger. One could hardly open a newspaper nowadays, much less a book of the lighter fiction, without reading of some kind of hijack. The word had become a platitude, which was more dangerous than the act itself.

Even the Captain avoided it carefully. Again he spoke briefly in Hebrew first and then in a much more fluent English.

'Ladies and Gentlemen, kindly listen. Three persons are trying to take over this aircraft. One is probably dead but two others are covering you. I beg you to do nothing foolish. Keep your seats and do as you're asked without question. On no account risk your lives by heroics. I am still in control of this aircraft completely and also in touch with Control on the ground. We shall be landing at Ben Gurion in what I estimate at forty-five minutes.'

Ben Gurion, Russell thought with amusement. Up to recently they had called it Lod for a living man's name could not be given to any public place or building. Now there were Ben Gurion Streets, a Ben Gurion Square and even an airport. Charles Russell accepted these facts indifferently for he knew that whatever honours were granted arrived on a man's head far too late and usually for irrelevant reasons. He looked at the handsome woman beside him. She was breathing evenly, alert but unfrightened. She wasn't going to lose her head. He asked into the eerie silence:

'What happens now?'

'We fly on to Ben Gurion.'

'In one piece?'

She shrugged. 'That depends on them.'

The woman in the nurse's uniform heard them talking and for the first time uttered. 'Silence at the back there. Quiet.' It had the slap of the hand which held a weapon but silence wasn't really necessary for her purpose of keeping the passengers seated. This woman had nerves like any other and she'd given Charles Russell a sudden idea. She was clearly the boss and wouldn't move, but if the man with the gun could be lured down the gangway, away from the cover of seated passengers, offering that spurious Rabbi a snapshot . . .

He said in a loud, clear, pompous voice:

'This is an outrage. I shall protest to my Consul.'

'Silence,' the nurse said again. 'Be quiet.'

'I repeat that I shall complain to my Consul.'

The nurse couldn't resist the sarcastic answer. 'Much good may that do you.'

'Then I'll see the Ambassador.'

The stewardess at Russell's side was more than a little disappointed. This man had had an air of authority, the manner of a man of the world, and here he was mouthing evident rubbish, the language of a gunboat diplomacy without the gunboats to back the peacock diplomats. She said in a sharp annoyance:

'Cut it.'

He looked at her, feigning offence, and went on. 'When we land in Israel——'

'*If* you land.' The nurse had suddenly lost her temper, this braying ass was stretching her nerves. She said to the doctor beside her:

'Quieten him.'

'Is it wise at this stage?'

'I said to quieten him.'

The doctor began to move down the aisle and Russell went on protesting senselessly. He was too wary to move his eyes from the nurse but from the corner of them he could see the Rabbi.

It happened as high class gunplay did, two shots which were almost but not quite together. The doctor staggered, then fell face forward. The Rabbi was still in his gangway seat and for a moment he stayed there, limp and unmoving. He tried to rise, then he too fell. He fell across the doctor's body. His black hat came off and his monstrous beard. Russell could see he was quite a young man.

On the flight deck the Third Officer had switched to one of his other cameras and the picture on his screen was clear again. The Captain was still watching it closely and this time he said:

'And then there was one.'

'But one with two grenades.'

'Just so.'

The stewardess in the seat beside Russell put her hand on his thigh and squeezed it gently. He was too sensible to suspect an advance and in any case the words which followed would have dashed conceit into instant fragments.

'I owe you an apology.'

'Why?'

'When you were going on like that I thought you were a silly old fuddy. Instead I find you're as smart as Satan.'

'Lucky too,' Russell said.

'I suppose you are. If he'd reached you he'd have shut your mouth.'

Russell hadn't meant that though the risk had been

there; he looked at the fallen Rabbi. 'I'm sorry.'

'I suppose he's really dead?'

'I'm afraid so. In any case we couldn't help him.' Russell's eyes moved away from the beardless Rabbi to the body in the front of the aircraft. Like the doctor and Rabbi it hadn't moved, but it hadn't been the noise of a shot which had woken Charles Russell from peaceful sleep but the scream of an hysterical woman. He saw that the stewardess had followed his look.

'How did he die?'

'Of shock. I mean it. That door can be electrified. Plenty.'

'All of it?'

'I don't know that.'

Nor, Russell thought, would the nurse with her hand grenades. The attendant's body was still touching the door: in turn she would hardly dare touch him for his gun. The doctor too had had a gun but he was ten paces down the aircraft's aisle and if she moved to him she'd expose her back to a lightning shot from a man on the flight deck. Her options had dwindled down to one, which was to throw a grenade, achieving nothing. And she didn't look a stupid woman, she must have guessed that every move she made was being followed on the closed circuit cameras.

An interesting situation. Russell wondered what he would do himself. He looked at the nurse again more closely. He wasn't interested in the fringe of black hair, in the glasses or the abrasive manner: they were the uniform of a certain ethos. He was interested in the woman who wore it. They would have trained her very thoroughly before they put her onto a mission like this and probably they had made her kill before they'd given her what was clearly its leadership; but you could never be sure of training anyone to cope with the totally unexpected. As this woman must do — the affair had gone sour on her. In that case all training became irrelevant, you were back upon individual character. He said to the stewardess sitting beside him:

'Do you think she can hear what we say?'

'She can hear that we are talking all right.'

As she proved she could for she shouted again. 'Silence at the back there. I mean it.'

This time Russell was more than just interested for she'd given an unenforceable order. Which was something no trained man ever did unless pressure had started to sap his judgement.

Charles Russell paid no attention to this but continued his conversation smoothly. 'I don't mind her hearing the fact that we're talking but she'd better not understand what we say. I think that you can speak Italian.'

'How did you guess?'

'It wasn't difficult.'

She had answered in a broad Neapolitan but Russell was able to follow her meaning. 'What do you think that woman wants?'

'Prisoners of her sort whom we're holding. And maybe some money as well for the next time.'

'She won't get either?'

'We won't even ask her.'

Charles Russell thought this over carefully, considering how he'd react himself if he wasn't even allowed to make his demand. He decided that it would add to the pressure, the sense of isolation and failure, the growing certainty it had all gone wrong. What he'd do then he didn't know, far less which side of the fence the nurse would fall.

The plane droned on through the afternoon and now silence sat on the cabin dourly. It was broken by a woman's voice, calling pleadingly to the dark-fringed nurse.

'My little boy wants the loo.'

'Impossible.'

'But he's in distress.'

'He can do the other thing.'

A silence again, then the voice of the boy.

'I'm sorry, mummy.'

'It wasn't your fault.'

Charles Russell had listened again intently for there was a message in this brief exchange for a man with a knowledge of human nature. The nurse was feeling the pressure increasingly. What risk could there be in a child of four walking back to the loos alone and returning? A woman who'd felt secure would have let him go. This one had not and that was significant.

The plane had begun to lose height for landing and the Captain's voice came over again. 'We shall be landing in a matter of minutes. Fasten your seat belts and do not smoke. On no account try to leave the aircraft.'

The inescapable funny man said: 'I wasn't going to.'

Nobody laughed. It wasn't funny.

The Captain brought her down quite normally. They taxied to a stop and he cut. Charles Russell looked out of the window again. All airports wherever they be looked much the same, distinguishable only by size and sometimes by a lighted sign. This one was rather more raw than many but evidently it was very efficient. Russell could see two half-tracks with troops in them and an armoured car with its cannon pointed, below it a co-axial machine gun.

A new voice came over the aircraft's speakers. It gave its name and rank in Hebrew, then changed to a correct cold English.

'I should make it clear that we're not prepared even to discuss your demands. Anything else you may wish to say will be relayed to me by the aircraft's Captain.'

The woman had begun to tremble — not violently, she was still controlling it. But Charles Russell could see she had nearly broken.

Which by no means meant that she wouldn't throw.

There was a mounting tension: the nurse stayed silent. At last she said:

'I've got grenades.'

'I know you have.'

'If you storm the aircraft I'll use them.'

'Possibly.' The voice was still cold and almost impersonal, the voice of a man who knew his duty and would be backed without question if forced to do it.

Russell wondered again what he'd do himself this time if he stood in this calm soldier's shoes. A burst through the aircraft's roof perhaps, well above the seated passengers? But no, that would frighten nobody except the already frightened passengers. Pointless displays of force weren't fruitful. But whatever happened would happen quickly. No bringing up teams of foreign psychiatrists to advise who might crack and when he would do so. There'd be a well-rehearsed procedure and they'd carry it out.

But there seemed to be one stage left before action. The cold voice went on as its orders required of it.

'And speaking of storming you mustn't think wrongly. We shan't have to fight our way in. We can walk. There are charges in all the doors already and the Captain, whom you can't reach, can fire them.'

Charles Russell nodded. They'd thought of everything.

The woman didn't answer this. She had a grenade in one hand but the hand wasn't steady. The Czech type, Russell saw. Quite deadly.

She was trembling uncontrollably now, fiddling with the grenade.

She dropped it.

There was another scream and a frozen silence but Russell was watching the nurse's hands. The pin was not in her fingers. Good. But she still had another and one would be plenty.

But no amount of training was absolute, sufficient for every contingency possible, and the nurse had moved far from the shadow of training. Instead of reaching for her second grenade she bent to recover the first from the floor. A man might have done it by flexing his knees, groping with his head still up and able to keep his eyes on the cabin. But that wasn't a woman's natural movement, and if she had ever been taught another the teaching had flown on the wind of her crisis. She went down on one knee and she lowered her head.

The man in the row of seats in front of her was elderly but still had sharp reflexes. As her head came down he grabbed her arms, pinning them to her sides in a bear hug. She struggled but he was still quite powerful. He pulled her head into his stomach and held her.

But not for long, he didn't need to. The door of the flight deck had opened instantly and a man had come out with an automatic. For a moment he considered coolly; he didn't want to wound a passenger. But he had a sideways shot through the woman's head.

He put his pistol into her ear and pulled.

Charles Russell said to the silent stewardess: 'I must thank you for a pleasant journey.'

It wasn't an irony for he hadn't been bored.

EIGHT

Charles Russell woke next morning uneasily, conscious that the day before him was unlikely to pass as he'd planned to pass it. Instead there'd be a string of statements to any official who cared to demand one and the Press in a mobbing *mêlée* with cameras. . . . 'Are you by any chance *the* Colonel Russell?' He shuddered but he couldn't avoid it.

But as it happened he didn't need to avoid it since it didn't arrive to invite avoidance. He owed this relief to Joe Beholden who'd been talking to his boss with some urgency. 'We owe him a little peace,' he had said. 'He helped us once and he did it handsomely. We ought to keep the Press off his back, and as for details of what really happened there's the crew and other Israeli citizens whom it would be reasonable to start on first. Later if there are particular points no doubt he'll be perfectly willing to clear them but for the moment I think we should let him be and moreover make sure that he isn't pestered.'

Beholden's boss had thought it over; he made his decisions slowly but stuck to them. 'Very well,' he had said. 'Send a man to see to it. But it would be rude not to call at all. Go later. But we'll give him a bit of time to find his feet.'

So Charles Russell went down to his breakfast uncertainly, expecting the worst but discovering nothing. There was a man in the foyer who wished him good morning but beyond the glass doors were no waiting reporters, no sign of even a single camera. He went into the restaurant, choosing his breakfast with cautious care. He had been told that an Israeli breakfast was something like a Dutch one but ampler, and with the ampler he was prepared to agree. He pecked at some toast and some mis-scrambled egg, relieved that the coffee at least was excellent.

He returned to the hall of his modest hotel and the man who had greeted him earlier rose at once.

'Colonel Charles Russell?'

'My name is Charles Russell.'

'I came here to try to save you annoyance.'

'That's extremely kind.' Russell looked around. 'I can see that it is also efficient.'

The man smiled and shrugged. 'We're efficient all right. Israel is a sort of democracy, the Press can print much what it likes and does, but when it comes to preventing it pestering visitors we have means which I rather think you have not.'

Charles Russell smiled in turn; he was liking this man. He hadn't yet met an Israeli politico, but Israeli officials — Joe Beholden, for instance — were frank to the point of inviting embarrassment. Charles Russell was not embarrassed but thankful.

'There's a matter in which you could help me.'

'Certainly.'

'I need to change a little money.'

'Then I advise you to proceed with caution.'

'But I'll need some Israeli money to move about.'

The other man waved at a desk in the corner. 'That's a bank. The rate that girl gives you is more or less right, allowing for the fact that it's phony, but don't change too much at a single time.'

'I'm very much obliged.'

'Not at all. And here's my card and a number to telephone. Just in case anyone happens to bother you.'

Charles Russell went to the corner table and sat down in front of the girl behind it.

'I'm afraid I don't speak Hebrew.'

'Nor do I as it happens, or not very well. They gave me a crash course — they give that to everyone — but my mother and father still speak English.'

'You're not a sabra, then?'

'I was born in South Africa.'

'Johannesburg?' It had seemed a good bet. She surprised him by saying:

'Potchefstroom.'

'Really?'

'And if you're wondering what Jews were doing in Potchefstroom we were keeping a shop and making a living. We were until my father spoke foolishly. Then nobody came to the shop any more. It was as simple as that. The business folded.'

He didn't answer since he understood perfectly; he changed thirty English pounds to Israeli money. She gave him the rate which was shown on her table.

'You like it in Israel?'

'I mean to stay here.'

'That doesn't answer my question.'

'Why should I answer it?' She spoke the words lightly but looked at him seriously. 'You must remember that we came from South Africa.'

Russell thanked her and walked to Ben Yahuda Street. He took a Number Four bus to the central bus station, for in any strange town he had one firm rule. He looked at the poorer quarter first, the slums if the word were not too outdated. These gave a city's authentic flavour undiluted by well-found hotels for tourists or the business quarter which might be anywhere.

He got down from his bus and looked around him, seeing that his instinct had been right. This was a different world entirely, the people in the streets *sephardim*. The predominant language seemed to be Hebrew but behind it was an eddy of Arabic, and as he warily probed the maze of alleys they might have been any *souk* on earth from Baghdad through the bad lands to Casablanca.

He had a map of a sort but was very soon lost. It didn't trouble him and he wandered on. Every ten paces he saw a soldier, shockingly, almost purposefully scruffy, his cap under his shoulder strap, his trousers unpressed, his boots unpolished. He looked like a brigand in looted uniform, but Russell had been a military radical and he knew you could make a fighting man without too much bawling on barrack squares. And how these young men had fought for their country!

But nation? He was less sure about that. He'd been reading up on the new biology and some of its jargon had stuck in his mind. The territorial imperative obviously operated but perhaps this was a *noyau* still, a place where you kept apart from your neighbours but never even considered attacking them since the enemy you shared in common was vastly more powerful and vastly more dangerous. Yet it was certain that few western Jews would give a daughter to one of these dark little warriors, and none of these superb little soldiers would fancy a woman of education. He had heard it said, and half believed it, that if the Arabs were really smart they'd make peace. Relieved of the pressure of outside hatred Israel would fall in pieces under their eyes. It might well, he reflected, do that in any case. In the Tel Aviv, which he'd left that morning, you seldom saw a pregnant woman. Here one in five was happily carrying.

He was lost but used his sense of direction, working his way what his guts said was north. He found a cruising taxi and stopped it, pointing to his hotel on the map. To his astonishment the driver spoke English.

'You are English, sir?'

.... Do I look all that English?

'I'm English all right.'

'I speak it too. I served in the Palestinian Police. I'm an Arab so I have many enemies. I thought you betrayed us, I think so still. But I will drive you to your hotel since I must.'

Russell climbed in and spread his map. Quite soon he picked his bearings up and, wise in the ways of taximen in any city on earth, said sharply:

'This isn't the way.'

'I know it, sir. I have something to show you. No extra charge whatever. Nothing.'

The insult was delivered smoothly by a man who knew his mind and would speak it. It would be foolish and maybe risky to protest. Russell sat silent and read his map. He could see they were going south, not north, but he doubted that he was being kidnapped. The driver had an air of malice but he hadn't the manner of active villainy.

They stopped in a crumbling and brokendown area

where the houses were being cleared for rebuilding and the rubble being dumped in the sea as foundations for a new esplanade. To the south was a high new hotel, still unfinished, another fly trap for the tourist with money, and beyond that again was the old town of Jaffa, now changed from a decayed sort of elegance to the brash chi-chi of international smartness. But where they had stopped said 'Street fighting' clearly, as Russell knew already there had been. The driver pointed at a ruined mosque.

'They smashed that,' he said. His voice was trembling.

Charles Russell was too wise to reply. The men who had attacked this area had been a breakaway group from a murderous gang but they hadn't attacked for the lust of destruction; they'd come in because in this seething cauldron no Jew could move without risking a sniper. They'd been everywhere and they'd been utterly merciless.

Russell looked again at the mosque with interest. Obviously it had been manned and defended and the raiders had brought their home-made artillery, something between a gun and a rocket. Its scars were unmistakable, the characteristic blackened hole. So this mosque had been manned and stoutly defended and the defenders had had to be winkled out.

Russell said ambiguously: 'I think I have seen enough for today.'

They drove back to his hotel in silence and Russell handed the Arab the full fare on the meter. He accepted it with a shrug, without thanks. He was prepared to insult a foreigner grossly but he wasn't prepared to refuse his money.

Russell saw that it was twelve o'clock — Lynne Hammer would have done her shopping. He telephoned and she answered at once. 'Good morning, Charles. I heard you were safe.'

He said a little testily: 'Everybody is perfectly safe except for some fools who asked for trouble and an unfortunate guard who did his duty.'

'Don't jump down my throat, I've had trouble myself.'

'What sort of trouble?'

'Oh, moving. Just moving. You won't want to hear the details, though. The important thing is I'm up to schedule.'

A remarkable woman, he thought — remarkable. He would have listened to those details with sympathy, the seamstress who had ruined the curtains, the carpet-layers who hadn't come. But no, just: 'I'm up to schedule.'

'Are you there still?'

'I was waiting for you.'

'This hotel isn't bad.'

'"Isn't bad"?' That sounds terrible. But I'll collect you in forty-eight hours. That suit you?'

'You're sure I won't——'

'I'm sure you won't. At midday on Friday then. That convenient?'

'Perfectly, thank you.'

'Then amuse yourself till then.'

She rang off.

Charles Russell ate his lunch reflectively. It was better than breakfast but not very much. The cooking, he assumed, was kosher, though he couldn't tell the difference by taste. But boiled chicken with the skin on was sickening and rice should be served with each grain separate, not slapped down on a plate in a soggy mass. Lynne's cooking would be simple but good.

After lunch he took his usual nap and awaking decided he'd go for a swim. He'd been warned that the sea itself was doubtful and though the seawater pool was clean and filtered it would also, at this hour, be crowded. But his hotel had a freshwater pool and he used it. He swam well, without fuss, in an easy crawl, turning at the ends professionally. He was enjoying a swim, not showing off, but he'd have had to be something less than human not to notice that there were others admiring him.

He dried himself and went back to his room. He had the latest book on a famous traitor and much of it made Charles Russell laugh. He also had a little whisky for he'd brazenly brought in more than one bottle. But he'd have to treat it carefully; he couldn't drink Lynne out of house and home for he didn't dare guess what its price would be locally.

He read till the day began to fade and his swim had made him hungry early. He couldn't face the hotel's dinner so he walked to the square by the sea and looked round. It was full of cafés selling pizza and Charles Russell had a taste for pizza. Moreover these looked good. He sat down.

The menu was in a bastard Italian and when the waitress came up he tried her in that.

'I'm sorry I can't speak Italian. Spanish.'

'I'm sorry I can't speak Spanish.'

'A pity. I love to speak it and hear it spoken.'

'You're Spanish, then?'

'No, Argentinian. Mendoza, as it happens. Beautiful. But I had to come here with my parents. They're old.'

He asked a question he'd asked once before that day. 'You like it here?'

She stared at him dumbly, silent and stricken. She had a look which he'd seen before in animals, in animals behind bars or in traps. Finally she said deliberately:

'I'd do anything in the world to get home.'

He could see that she was speaking literally. If he offered the air fare to Buenos Aires she'd do anything in the world to earn it.

He was a man who liked his chores behind him, so next morning he walked to Ben Yahuda again, to his travel agency to check his flight home. His agency had fussed about that and Charles Russell suspected a tiresome formality. Nevertheless they'd insisted, so he would go.

The man behind the desk rose at once. 'How can I help you, sir?'

'This ticket. I'm told that I have to check the flight home.'

'I'll do that with pleasure.'

He did so, in English. Plenty of people in Israel spoke English but this was a very English English; it could only have been learnt from an Englishman. 'You were born in England?' Charles Russell asked.

'No, not at all, I was born in Palestine.' He pointed at the plaque on his desk. 'Benjamin Gordon my name is, sir.' He pronounced it the Israeli way. 'You mustn't suppose I have Scottish blood. My parents came from a Baltic state and in a way I suppose I'm a sort of aristocrat. The Gordons were famous pioneers.'

He was clearly more than willing to talk so Russell went on. 'But that English of yours——'

'I learnt it in the British army, where I enlisted in the last stupid war. I say stupid because you lost the peace. The Royal Corps of Transport they call it now but then it had a ruder nickname.' He added with an evident pride. 'I must be one of very few Israelis who rose to the rank of sergeant major in a regular British army unit. That was tougher than getting an easy commission.'

'Indeed it was,' Charles Russell said. He said it with a real respect.

'You were in the army yourself, sir?'

'Once I was. I got shunted off to other duties.'

The travel clerk took this without a blink for he'd learnt that many British Regulars had interests other than merely soldiering. Or had had: it was different now. 'You're on a visit here?'

'I was here in the Troubles. I thought that I'd like to see it again.'

'You notice differences?'

'Very great differences.'

'You read the local papers?'

'I can't.'

'I meant the local papers in English.'

'I haven't had time to look at them yet.'

'Then you shouldn't believe a word they say.'

'In what particular way should I read with reserve?'

'This business of the Settlements.'

'Yes? You mean the Settlements in the recovered

territories?' He'd been careful not to use the word 'occupied'.

'I don't say we won't hold on to a few in the areas where they're strategically necessary — trained soldiers masquerading as farmers. But the rest of it is a kind of game, a game we play with President Carter. He tells us we're naughty boys to colonize, so we draw back a little and Carter is happy; he lets us have our money and guns. Particularly the money, sir. Every man and woman and child in this country is subsidized by American money to the tune of five hundred sterling pounds annually. Without it we should starve as we stand and without their arms we'd be sitting ducks.'

'But I thought you had a policy——'

'*Aliyah*, you mean?'

'Whatever's that?'

'It means unrestricted immigration and it's as out of date as last year's pop tunes. Massive settlement is out of the question. They never publish the figures of course, but my guess is that we're losing men net. More Jews are going out than coming in. As for Russian Jews, that's a foolish pipe dream. Russia isn't going to oblige an enemy by giving it what it needs most next to money, and as for the trickle she does let out, half of them never reach Israel anyway. They drop off in Vienna and stay there comfortably. We only keep our figures up because the oriental Jews breed like rabbits. Quite soon we'll be a sephardic state if the Arabs don't strangle us first. As they may.'

Charles Russell rose. 'We must talk again.'

'At any time you fancy, sir.'

At his hotel he decided to skip his lunch and in his bedroom the telephone woke him at three.

'There's a gentleman to see you, sir.'

'What's his name?'

'Mr Joseph Beholden.'

'Please ask him to come up to my room.'

It was far too hot to need to dress and Russell chose a dressing gown, smiling at the irreverent thought that he was going to hold a sort of levée. Joe Beholden came in and shook hands warmly. 'I hope I didn't wake you.'

'No matter.'

Joe Beholden, as Russell knew, was blunt, and he said at once: 'I told you so.'

'That I was accident prone? The affair of that aircraft?'

'It proved my point.'

'It did no such thing. I beg to distinguish, I really must. Agreed that that aircraft met with an accident but that accident wasn't directed at me. You cannot conclude that a man's prone to accidents when several hundred others were also involved.'

'Too subtle for me,' Joe Beholden said.

Charles Russell changed the subject smoothly. 'I take it that I owe it to you that I haven't been pestered to death by the Press.'

'We did make certain arrangements — yes. So I've come to ask for a *quid pro quo*.'

'Reasonable.'

'We think so too. So we'd rather you didn't contact the Admiral.'

'We had that rubbish out in London.'

'And with respect I don't think you quite took the

point. Naturally we don't suppose that you'd go in with any plan of his but we do believe he has something cooking — I told you he suffered from Hero's Disease — and if he somehow caused a crisis locally the mere fact that a Colonel Charles Russell had met him——'

'You overrate Colonel Charles Russell absurdly.'

'—— would be something which the Press would leap at. Any journalist of any competence could brew up a pretty sinister story.'

'I thought you had your Press sewn up.'

'We can prevent it annoying distinguished visitors, but believe it or not this is still a democracy.'

Charles Russell let this pass unsmiling, and Beholden went on on a note of urgency. 'Then think of your own Ministers too — the embarrassment, perhaps even the scandal. If you won't think of *my* country think of your own.'

'I'd very much rather not.'

'Why's that?' Joe Beholden was surprised and showed it.

'I'm a marxist,' Charles Russell said.

'A *what?*'

'Not the whole way, of course — by no means. But I've accepted one of its basic premises. We live in an age of naked class warfare, and accepting that fact a word like "country" is poor guidance in one's daily decisions.' He hesitated but added finally. 'I realize that I have more in common with a German doctor in private practice than with an Englishman in a coal mine in Durham.'

'You amaze me, sir,' Joe Beholden said.

'Sometimes I amaze myself. But I try to keep in

touch with reality.'

'Then you still mean to meet our respected Admiral?'

'I will if he invites me to.'

'Has he?'

Joe Beholden had barked it a trifle brusquely but Russell was in no way offended. Joe Beholden was very smart indeed but nobody would have insulted him by accusing him of sensitivity. So Russell began to explain urbanely.

'If you mean have I telephoned? no, I haven't. I could hardly arrive unannounced in Israel and telephone after thirty years. It's true that we exchange cards of greeting but I do that to several dozen people whom I wouldn't know if I met them casually and to many more as a matter of courtesy whom I never want to see again. So I wrote him a little letter from England. That was something over ten days ago and so far he hasn't written or telephoned though I told him where I'd be staying in Tel Aviv.'

Russell rang for tea and when it came poured it. Joe Beholden's manner unexpectedly hardened.

'You realize what all this means?'

'You tell me.'

'I'll be frank with you.'

'I prefer it that way.' Charles Russell was telling the truth; he did.

'We don't know in detail what that Admiral's plotting though we've infiltrated his immediate circle. We employ his favourite confidant and what he's told us so far is sufficiently serious.'

'Sufficiently for what?'

'Sufficient to have to watch the Admiral.'

Charles Russell took the point at once. 'Which means that if I meet him you'll watch me too. If I meet him in a public place there'll be somebody there to make a tape, and if I meet him in his house or here you'll arrange for a suitable bug to record us.'

'Wouldn't you do the same?'

'Perhaps.'

'You realize it's an embarrassment?'

'Yes.'

'Won't you spare us that embarrassment?'

'No.'

'I still think you're prone to accidents, Colonel.'

Again Charles Russell didn't smile. 'And this time that's a delicate threat?'

'Take it as you please.'

'I shall.'

Joe Beholden rose and took his leave. He'd have to report to his boss at once.

NINE

Joe Beholden's boss, like the Admiral himself, had somehow escaped the Nazi terror. He was a European Jew unmistakably, and an English Jew would have guessed he was German. He was powerfully built with a strong thick neck and he wore his almost white hair *en brosse*. He was also a deeply religious man who belonged to a 'Religious' party, and a Talmudic scholar of solid repute. In private life he was gentle and generous but in the service of the state of Israel no holds were barred, he was wholly unscrupulous. Joe Beholden respected but didn't much like him for they came from very different backgrounds. Not that that fact was important: both were Jews. He said to Joe Beholden crisply:

'And what did you get from calling on Russell?'

'Nothing. I'd told him in London the Admiral was dangerous, brewing up something which might be deadly. It would be embarrassing if anything broke, but doubly so if it got around that Colonel Russell had been meeting our Admiral. Even worse if some newspaper chose to plug it.'

'And what did he say?'

'He wouldn't budge.'

'You do not surprise me.'

The boss smiled dourly; he'd met Charles Russell. He was a very easy man to work with once he'd made

p his mind you had interests in common, but he
'asn't one to forgo a project because you gave him
alf a reason to do so.

Half a reason — that was the difficulty. They had
ifiltrated the Admiral's organization — no, coterie
'as a better word — but they still didn't know his
xact intention or even if he really had one. He didn't
ossess effective power, neither in a political party nor
et with a disciplined underground. Time had washed
im up on a beach and left him, a disappointed but still
angerous man, for he still had men who would follow
im blindly and the sons of those men might do the
ame.

But follow him blindly in what? God knew. He
ouldn't control events, that was certain. Indeed he
ad failed once already to do so when a premature
oup in Alidra had broken and that friend of his, Rifai,
ad gone under. That plan was dead. But the Admiral
ad never surrendered easily; he might seize on some
hance incident and fan it into the fire of crisis, some
utrage which could destroy his country. And with the
Middle East as it was today, a football between com-
eting Powers, no man could say with a hope of convic-
ion that such an incident wouldn't occur tomorrow.

'We'll have to put the real bite on Ben Arie.'

Joe Beholden liked the sound of that for Ben Arie
vas a man he detested. He despised all traitors, espe-
ially private ones, and Ben Arie had been one of the
Admiral's officers. To Joe Beholden that made it
vorse.

A squalid tale, he reflected glumly. Ben Arie, like
he Admiral, had gone into politics after the wars, but
inlike the Admiral he'd been highly successful. He was

115

high in his party, the same as the boss's, though it wa
known he was a bitter sceptic; he'd been a member o
the Knesset for years, and if the right sort of coalitio
came up he'd certainly become a Minister. But ala
he'd been greedy and paid the price. An English-lan
guage newspaper had recently put it neatly but oddly

*The amateur public which is buying shares at th
Stock Exchange thinks the rates move in one directio
only: upwards — and this is their mistake.*

Ben Arie had gone in deeper and deeper, first on hi
own money, then on borrowed. When the break cam
he was effectively bankrupt. He had gone to Behold
en's boss to save him for none of his own relation
could lend him more. He knew that this tough officia
despised him since he shouldn't be a 'Religious' at all
but the fact of their party in common remained and i
couldn't afford a resounding scandal. Beholden's bos
gave the minimum help which would prevent that scan
dal breaking openly, but the price of his twenty piece
of silver had been the traditional one of total betrayal
The Admiral trusted Ben Arie blindly, he went to hin
for advice almost daily, advice in the world of activ
politics which had used the Admiral, then droppe
him brutally.

The boss had seen Beholden's expression. He didn'
smile often and then somewhat wintrily but now hi
smile was understanding. He mistrusted the use o
informers on principle and in the Admiral's case it wa
also distasteful.

'I can see you don't like Ben Arie. Nor do I. He's al
the things which were once thrown at Jews, graspin
and corrupt and petty.'

'Israelis have outgrown the ghetto.'

'I'm happy to say that's mostly true. All the worse or us when one reneges. So I had to save his face. At a rice. I hated giving him a single pound but in our profession one can't have scruples.'

'I'm not asking what you gave him, sir, but he's iven us very little lately, just some fantasy about natching a tanker which I suppose he'd made up to eep us quiet.'

'Then he'd better come up with something solid.' 'he voice was suddenly harsh and formidable. 'I'd like ou to warn him of that at once. Give him a couple of lays to find out what's really in the Admiral's mind.'

'You feel yourself there's something new?'

'Not certainly — not certainly formed. But anything ould happen tomorrow and the Admiral might see an pening.' Beholden's boss leant forward sharply. How senile do you think he is?'

Beholden repeated his statement to Russell. 'I don't hink he's senile at all — far from it. But he's a man rom a different age and climate and he isn't any longer oung. If the pressures built up ....' He left it unfinshed and started again. 'As you get older you can't tand much pressure.'

It wasn't the most tactful thing to say to a man himelf in his sixties, but Beholden's boss showed no esentment; he knew it to be perfectly true. He couldn't tand great pressures himself and in a year or two he'd e retiring and gladly.

'Then get to work on Ben Arie at once.'

'Immediately.'

'And Joe.'

Beholden hid his surprise successfully. His boss very eldom used given names.

'One other thing. Do you *know* the Admiral?'

'I've never had the honour of meeting him.'

'Do you admire him?'

'No, he's too dangerous.'

'Respect him?'

'Yes. Sincerely respect.'

Beholden's boss said very quietly: 'For your privat
information so do I.'

An oleander hedge gave a welcome shade and in it th
Sheikh and Rifai were chatting. For the Sheikh ha
discharged his promises scrupulously. Rifai must no
write to the Admiral — he didn't — and when th
Sheikh wished to talk, which was three times a week
Rifai must appear and do his duty. And they'd dis
covered another matter in common besides th
Sheikh's need to talk intelligently and this was the fac
that Rifai played tennis. The Sheikh had a profes
sional but the professional drove him near to dotty
Like the men the Sheikh's uncle had tried to play ches
with the professional wouldn't play it straight; he'
run the Sheikh round the court and then suddenl
lose. The Sheikh was no fool and he thought it a
insult. The man must know perfectly well he coul
beat him, and to throw the game away like a lacke
was something which was hard to bear. But with Rifa
he could have a proper game. Sometimes the Sheik
would win and sometimes not.

So they sat with soft drinks and chatted amiably
The Sheikh asked:

'How's that book coming on?'

'The one about Islam — the sin of drinking? The on

bout Christendom's horror of sex? It isn't coming on
t all. For one thing I lack the wit to write it and for
nother I found it's been done already. By an Anglican
lergyman of all things imaginable. And very well
lone at that. There's nothing left.'

'Then how do you pass your time?'

'I think a lot.'

'Planning another *coup d'état*?' The Sheikh had
miled as he asked the question.

Rifai shook his head.

'Then aren't you lonely?'

'Sometimes a little but not very much.'

'I'm lonely all the time,' the Sheikh said.

'When you married again there were loyal rejoic-
ngs.'

'For my part they were somewhat misplaced. Politi-
ally it was a very good match — she's a daughter of
ny feudal overlord. She's also extremely pious and
rthodox and a pious woman can be worse than a
hrew.'

'There's a rumour——'

'It is quite correct. The lady is undeniably pregnant
nd totally, almost indecently proud of it. I only hope
he bears a son.'

'So do we all.'

'You misunderstand me. If it isn't a son I must try
gain and that isn't a prospect I greatly fancy. In fact,
hough it's somewhat ungallant to say it, I'm begin-
ing to feel a certain sympathy for the tastes of my
amented uncle.'

'As bad as that?'

'She suffers me dutifully.'

The Sheikh gave Rifai a cigar and lit his own. 'Have

you ever had a happy liaison?'

'I was lucky. I was happily married.'

'And so was I for many years, though technically i
wasn't a marriage. Have you ever heard of Mrs Lynn
Hammer?'

'Should I have heard?'

'No, I don't think you should. In any case she's i
Israel now.'

'Israel?' He didn't believe his ears. The ex-mistres
of the Sheikh in Israel . . . .

The Sheikh saw his confusion and laughed at i
gently. 'Oh yes, she was a Jewess all right but only i
the most technical sense. She wasn't born in Israel, yo
see, but deep in the American heartland. Nor were he
parents Jewish but Christian. But one grandmothe
was undeniably Jewish and she's the daughter of tha
grandmother's daughter.'

'I see,' Rifai said.

'But I doubt if you do. I couldn't have brought he
here of course, nor to any other Arab country. Som
prying fool would have nosed it out though she didn'
look like a Jewess and far less behave like one. But
took her everywhere else without a qualm.'

. . . .Without a qualm — a gross litotes. It had bee
very hard indeed to lose her. Like Charles Russell h
thought her a rare sort of woman. . . . Advise and Con
sent — now why had he thought of that? It was the con
stitutional relationship between the Senate and th
American President but it was seldom one betwee
man and wife. More likely that was Explain and Jus
tify. Answer all the questions patiently but know tha
you weren't advancing your cause. But Lynne Ham
mer had never been tainted with that. If you said tha

120

ou wanted to do a thing she either said yes or no, nostly yes. She even let a man read when she wanted o talk.

He'd been astonished when she'd written briefly tell-ng him she was settling in Israel. He'd never thought of her as a Jewess, never, and she'd never even men-ioned Zionism. He had no inkling of the goad which lad driven her, no insight into her private motive, but t was a comfort to know that in Israel she'd be eceived. Of course she'd be received; she had money. sraelis, he thought with an Arab's smile, were more han a little ambivalent on the subject of other Jews vith money. The enormously rich ones, the merchant rinces, had better stay away from Israel, visiting it ccasionally to plant trees and leave a million behind hem. But there was bitter and often open resentment hat other Jews stayed away in thousands, especially hose who'd made modest fortunes and were comfort-bly retired elsewhere. They went to Florida or the outh of France, to Majorca, or they stayed in their iouses. What right had they to flats in Majorca when heir comfortable hard currency incomes could under-in Israel's limping economy?

He decided it was a point of view; he didn't con-lemn, for he wasn't censorious, nor share his thoughts vith the man beside him. He had business to discuss vith him and being an Arab he went at it sideways.

'I gather, then, that you're not too bored.'

'I'd be happier with something to do.'

'You told me your intention once. You didn't mean o usurp my throne, only to have my ear and make use of it. I remember you even used the word Minister.'

'All that's behind me now for ever.'

'I'm not so sure — you're extremely intelligent. I can't keep you here for ever in idleness and I don't have so many intelligent men that I can afford to waste a potential asset.' He looked hard at Rifai. 'Would you like to work?'

'What sort of work?'

'I'd like you to slap down Oceanic.'

'The company which runs the oil?'

'The company which is trying to take me. Now listen very carefully, please.' He wasn't an Arab now but the cool tycoon. 'In its way its something more than ironical since in the average oil state it's the other way round; it's the state which is squeezing the foreign company, whittling away at the basic concession, asking for higher royalties — all the rest. But here it's Oceanic trying to squeeze *me*. They want much more oil for rather less money and they hold a pretty good hand to demand it. There's oil here but we're by no means a major — I don't compare with my new wife's father — and it might not tempt another consortium even if oil dog ate dog which it doesn't. Be that as it may it seems they are serious. They're going to have a try at me while I'm still dependent on men they lent me when your compatriots made a mess of it and got killed.'

The Sheikh had guessed that Rifai was interested and his question confirmed the impression promptly.

'How are you going to meet it?'

'How would you?'

'It would depend on what cards I held myself.'

'One ace. You know my uncle was very rich?'

'I'd always assumed he wasn't poor.'

'So had I but when he died he surprised me. Do you wish to know what he had?'

'If you care to say.'

The Sheikh named a figure and Rifai whistled. 'And not in some numbered account in Switzerland. It was in his own name and all over the world. Since I happen to be his heir it's now mine. I mean to use it against Oceanic.'

Rifai, as the Sheikh had said, was intelligent. 'You would tell them you could live without oil?'

'I could do that for at least two years, by which time their investment here would have crumbled into almost nothing. I'm not an extravagant man myself and the sum I've just mentioned is more than enough to pay the army and anything else essential for the two years till Oceanic is on its knees.'

'Quite a card,' Rifai said.

'Will you pick it up?'

Rifai appeared to be thinking it over though in fact he knew he needn't do so; he said at last:

'It doesn't seem I have much choice.'

'If you put it like that I suppose you haven't.' The Sheikh hadn't changed his voice or his manner but unmistakably he was speaking as master. He named a salary. 'Is that enough?'

'Princely. As befits a prince.'

'And you'll realize that this is a sort of trial. If you succeed in this important matter there's another which you mentioned before which I might be prepared to discuss again. *Might* be prepared. I am making no promises. But you're an unusual sort of Palestinian.'

'I take that as a compliment, sir.'

The Sheikh took a shower and dressed himself comfortably (comfortably meant western clothes), then he lay on a long cane chair and thought. He was dressed in comfortable western clothes but he was far from thinking western thoughts. He supposed he should go and visit his wife but he didn't much feel like her withering company. It was frustrating being an Arab prince, and not only in the matter of matrimony, making a marriage which wasn't congenial but simply to secure the succession. And there were other more onerous irritations, for instance that the oil Arabs sat on barely compensated for Arab incompetence. Especially for their military syncope. No doubt that was more than a little unfair since there'd always been Arabs who fought like tigers provided they were properly led by men whom they both liked and respected. But the lumpen levy was not like that. Perhaps it had improved a little from the level of what had been merely disgraceful, but it was still a poor match for determined patriots who fought with their backs to the open sea. So all one could do was to buy them arms, hoping they wouldn't lose the lot, knowing that in any battle they could afford the casualties, Israel could not. But that was the lowest form of warfare, the insanity of the first world war.

And when it came to political warfare oil was a weapon which cut both ways. An embargo had once frightened the West, but another might be strongly challenged. Pressed to the point of no return it might very well strangle the West's economy, but to whose profit would such an action be? It would exchange a dubious interdependence for a single and wholly ruthless master.

The Sheikh frowned in frustration, for the Sheikh was an Arab and he didn't believe that his peers had been clever. They'd made every mistake in the political book. It had looked so smart, so smart and slick, to back those preposterous Palestinians, insisting that they had only one home and that in the land they had recently left, fining some wretched man *in absentia* for selling his land in an occupied territory. There were thirteen states in the Arab League, of which nine could have absorbed these men without noticing they had lost an acre and with the knowledge that money from oil would come with them. Instead they'd been put in camps to rot. A political weapon? Yes, of a sort. But in their camps they had bred and festered and hated, turning as often as not against their hosts. Now they eddied round the Middle East like hot money round a western economy.

The Sheikh grunted and went to his solitary breakfast. He was certain his fellow princes had played it wrong. That man Rifai, he thought — he'd had a dream. Or was it a dream? He was half persuaded. But he wouldn't make his mind up at once. He'd watch how Rifai played Oceanic while he handled a second small matter himself, the disposal of his surviving prisoners. To try them publicly would offend other Arabs and he shrank from any coldblooded killing. So he'd have to let them escape discreetly and that was going to need careful handling.

TEN

The Admiral had had Russell's letter but decided he'd think it over before he replied. Russell could have written from courtesy or maybe to avoid embarrassment if the Admiral should hear he had visited Israel without making a gesture of simple friendliness. In one way he wanted to see him badly, but they hadn't met for thirty years and to try to go back in time could disappoint.

He walked across the road to think of it, sitting on a rock on his knoll. The heat of the stone warmed his bottom comfortably and the view warmed his heart as it always had, the shimmering gleam of the Mosque of the Rock, the walled city beyond it and then the new. He'd been born in another continent, but this was now his town, his own. It had been bought in a savage and bitter battle and would never be given up but by conquest. It would certainly never be put under tutelage to men from some soulless impersonal sham, to overpaid Scandinavians who couldn't be trusted to fight a baby and to Irishmen who fought only each other.

So should he ask Russell here, to his flat? He wasn't ashamed of his small neat flat and Russell was a man of the world who would know that in the State of Israel a retired official, however senior, seldom had more than his pension to· live on. Charles Russell would not expect a state banquet.

But there were other and more domestic difficulties. His wife was not having an easy pregnancy and he'd been warned there might be complications. The doctor was calling almost daily, and though he hadn't said so in terms the Admiral had a strong suspicion that a hospital bed was kept ready and waiting. No, he couldn't ask Russell to come to Jerusalem.

Particularly not with that man outside his home. He hadn't followed him to his rock on the hillside since this evening stroll was established routine, but when the Admiral returned he'd still be there. He couldn't risk inviting Russell to a home which was plainly under surveillance. That would be a humiliation. Russell had been in that business himself and even if he didn't see some instinct might convey the message. The Admiral couldn't face that and he wouldn't.

He decided to go to Tel Aviv, to meet Russell on neutral ground, in a café. Of course that damned shadow would follow him there but he wouldn't attempt to conceal his presence: on the contrary he would point him out, explaining that he was his personal bodyguard. Since this could have been the simple truth, since there'd been two attempts on his life already, he believed that he could lie with conviction. Russell would almost surely accept it, humiliation would be neatly avoided. With a man outside in the street it could not.

He returned to his flat and wrote to Russell but he wrote with a certain reserve and caution. He knew that men of Russell's background often fancied a couple of gins before lunch but the Admiral didn't propose to buy them. It wasn't that he was mean by nature, it was simply he'd little taste for alcohol and gin in particular made him queasy. So he named a café in Dizengoff Street and a time at ten o'clock in the morning. That would involve a couple of coffees, and cakes if Charles Russell ate cake in the morning. For all of these he would pay very happily.

He slipped out to post his handwritten letter and this time the man outside did follow. The Admiral paid him no attention: he'd have nothing to report again.

He went back again to talk to his wife but she was resting and he didn't disturb her. Instead he went to his den to think.

The view from his rock had lifted his heart for this was territory which had been bought with blood; but also it had saddened him for it was territory under seige. They'd win the next war and the one after that but each of them would mean taking casualties and the brute facts of population were hostile. But give them the oil which they hadn't got, give them the independence of owning it . . . .

He'd had a good plan once and chance had destroyed it, the chance that Rifai had arrived too late. He frowned for he'd been hoping foolishly, hoping against all logic and reason that one day the Pole would appear in the garden with a message across his now silent channel . . . . Rifai was alive after all and working . . . . Nonsense, the man Rifai was dead. The Admiral sincerely hoped he was dead since he knew what one Arab could do to another.

He nodded for he was almost asleep, but in the penumbra between sleep and waking his brain had always worked with clarity. This second plan of his. . . . . He grunted. He had mentioned it to Ben Arie once, who had stared and then concealed a smile. Clearly he hadn't taken it seriously. Yes, he had said, he supposed it was on — on as a sort of Staff College exercise. But it was betting against the odds alarmingly. Too many movements would have to coincide.

The Admiral had gone silent at once, not disclosing that the spadework had been done.

At this moment, half in sleep, half waking, the Admiral was inclined to agree. Some event might force his hand to action as the flow and neap of war had done in the past, but for the moment he was no longer young, he was content to run with the tide and await his chance. Life was another war — what else?

The old Admiral was fast asleep.

Ben Arie was not; he was thinking hard. He wanted Beholden's boss off his back and in one respect he was free to throw him. A legacy from an American cousin had cooled the worst of the fire beneath his feet. He wasn't going to repay his family, he considered them fools to have lent unsecured, but he could pay off his commercial creditors, he could avoid an immediate and crushing bankruptcy. He could tell Beholden's boss to go to hell.

Except that he could do no such thing since Beholden's boss would always *know* and in a puritanical state such knowledge stuck. A Minister had had to resign for little more than a breach of Exchange Control and his own party waved a lilywhite banner. It would be bad that he'd been gambling heavily; it would be worse that it would be said at once that he'd bought shares which no politician should. Beholden's boss held the whip for ever, but he held it through the Admiral, his need to know what the old man was brewing. Therefore if the Admiral weren't there. . . .

If the Admiral weren't there he'd be shot of his chains.

He'd been expecting another call from Beholden for he knew that he hadn't been earning his money. That story about snatching a tanker. He hadn't taken it as serious planning but had passed it over to keep them quiet. So far it had but it wouldn't for long.

His quick corrupt mind saw the opening instantly. If the story were less fantastic, more likely, if some flesh could be put on improbable bones. . . .

As a politician he had excellent contacts and he used them without exposing his interest. The answers to his inquiries made him smile. So that Admiral had his connections still, the fantasy had some roots in fact.

When Beholden called he received him coolly but he contrived to look both solemn and frightened. Beholden took a taxi back. He couldn't charge it — they were mean with expenses — but he had to see his boss at once.

Ben Arie went out and bought himself dinner at a restaurant his party would not have approved of. He settled in foreign currency which he wasn't supposed to have but did. He then took a hostess back to his flat, paying her forty per cent of what he'd agreed.

Joe Beholden could see he'd thrown a thunderbolt. His boss was an impassive man and in his work he had very good reason to be so but he was holding on to control with difficulty. He coughed twice and blew his nose, then said:

'I suppose this is true?'

'We can check, of course. But I think it's too detailed for simple fiction.'

'A tanker of a hundred thousand, due at Alidra on Friday morning and flying a flag of convenience.'

'Easily verified.'

'Do so. And then?'

'Of the coastal patrol boats now in Eilat two have Captains who once served the Admiral. And one of the two boats carries missiles.'

'What do you think?'

'I don't know what to.'

Beholden's boss said grimly: 'I asked you.'

'It would be lunatic and the Admiral isn't.'

'You said that before.'

'And I'm going to stick to it. But under pressure he might crack. They all do.'

The boss did not pursue the 'they'. 'We could warn the Navy,' he said.

'No doubt. Who must then arrest two senior Captains and hold them *incommunicados* till a tanker has loaded and sailed away. With that sort of ship that's a week at least and probably rather more than that. There couldn't be any question of charging them, just relieving them of command on suspicion. Do you think that could be kept quiet?'

'It might.'

'If it wasn't there'd be an immediate row.'

'Not as great as if the Admiral acted.'

They fell into an uncomfortable silence. Both men were smoking and neither did often. The boss said at length:

'Then how do you see it?'

'What the Admiral would do if indeed he did? With

two ships behind him he might do anything. He has some famous coups in his log already.'

'Another Entebbe?'

'Much worse than that. Entebbe was an official action, planned by Staff Officers and agreed by the Cabinet. Even so not every country approved of it. France, you remember, was actively hostile, but then the French will lick anyone's arse when it comes to a question of keeping their oil safe. But any unofficial action would put us in the dock for a decade.'

The boss thought this over, frowning unhappily. 'Then what sort of coup could this really be?'

'One of two. The crews of supertankers are surprisingly small, and people who serve under flags of convenience are very seldom fighting men. So he might let her sail and try to board her.'

'Which would be piracy of the grossest sort.' Beholden's boss continued disgustedly. 'And then I suppose he'd sail her to Eilat, presenting us smugly with pirated oil. Which he'd know, if he thought, that we couldn't accept. On the contrary we'd be in the wrong at once, repudiating the Admiral's action, apologizing humbly all round and paying God knows what in damages. So that's one of your coups. Now what's the other?'

'Or he might go for her while she's still tied up.'

'When the Alidran army would go for *him*. Which wouldn't mean international odium at a moment we can least afford it; it would mean an immediate war which might spread.' The boss corrected himself. 'Not might but would.'

Beholden was still smoking steadily. He hadn't wanted another, his mouth was fouled; he said but not in a tone of conviction:

'All this is still suspicion, sir.'

'A suspicion of the Admiral's state of mind. I think you said he might crack under pressure. Do you know of any such pressure?'

'Not really. His wife is having a difficult preg-nancy——'

The boss shook his head at once. 'Not enough.' He slipped back again into thought, then said: 'Only one thing in all this is sure. Nothing can happen without the Admiral and he's got to get down to Eilat himself to reach the only resources he has.'

'We might stop him.'

'How?'

'Perhaps what was once called protective cus-tody——'

Beholden's boss almost lost his temper, something Beholden had never yet seen, but equally he had never seen him in a dilemma bearing horns quite so pointed. 'I think that's a very stupid suggestion. To pull in our respected Admiral would be almost as bad as that oil at Eilat. It's true it would be a domestic scandal instead of an international uproar, but uproar there would be all right and I doubt if our masters would dare to back us.'

Joe Beholden knew that this was true. He was increasingly uneasy and nervous, tired of analysis, tired of talk. He wanted a decision quickly and it wasn't his business to make that decision. But he might bring it a little closer; he said:

'So what we're facing is an appalling risk.'

'You're telling me.'

'I'm not telling you, sir, I'm simply asking. Is it a risk you're prepared to accept?'

'You're pressing me rather.'

'Yes sir, I am.'

Beholden's boss rose and walked to the window. The view from it was not inspiring, another Institute for Talmudic Studies, yet another hotel for American tourists. Beholden could see his broad shoulders, the back of his head. It was a square like the caricature of a Prussian's, and Beholden knew he could act as ruthlessly. He stood there for some minutes silently, then returned to his desk and sat down deliberately.

'I think it was a splinter group which tried twice for the Admiral's life before.'

Beholden let his breath out at last: the decision had been taken wordlessly. He didn't approve it, he thought it regrettable, but he respected the man who could take it so calmly. The Admiral was a national hero but when it came to the state's essential interests he was as expendable as a private soldier.

The boss read his expression and hid a smile. So he needn't explain and he needn't justify; he need only ask the imperative questions.

'Do you know the Admiral's future movements?'

'He's meeting Charles Russell on Friday.'

'Where?'

'In a café in Tel Aviv.'

'You're sure?'

'Of course I'm sure. We read his mail.'

'At what time are they meeting?'

'At ten tomorrow.'

It was very short notice, too close for comfort, too close for reflection or indecision. But the boss had never been indecisive and his organization was highly tuned, Beholden himself in the top class of operators.

Moreover ten o'clock was convenient since the café itself would not be crowded. A waiter perhaps but nobody else for it was much before the hour of the coffee house. Not a chance to be lightly turned down and missed because the timing was notably less than leisurely. The boss thought for perhaps a minute, then said:

'You could fix it in the time available?'

'I've got what's left of today and the night to work in.'

'Enough, do you think?'

'With any luck.'

'Very well, go ahead.' There was a small relaxation but not a long one. 'You realize the essential, of course?'

'It must look like another job by some terrorist.'

'So you mustn't use an Israeli weapon which some explosives expert might ferret out afterwards. We have one of theirs?'

'We've captured plenty.'

'Russian, I suppose.'

'And Czech.'

'And if by some chance the café is crowded you have authority to call if off.'

'Thank you for that.'

'Are you being impertinent?'

'No sir, but I do have a question.'

'Ask your question, then.'

'The man who'll be with him, that man of our own.'

'No man of our own should be anywhere near him. You're to call him off for the day. And make sure of it.'

'He'll be able to draw conclusions afterwards.'

'What of it? Isn't the man secure?'

He'd be secure all right, Joe Beholden thought. There'd been a recent case where a man had talked idly and his car had run over a Syrian mine in an area which had been clear for years. His family had been with him too. Regrettable again, but necessary.

Beholden rose and walked to the door. At it he made a single comment.

'A pity about Charles Russell.'

'A pity.'

On Thursday Russell breakfasted quietly, looking forward to his move to Lynne's next day. He had never much cared for life in hotels. In the foyer the desk clerk gave him his mail, a single letter with a Jerusalem postmark. It was an answer from the Admiral and it suggested a meeting at ten next morning, naming a café in Dizengoff Street. Russell was a little surprised, less at the choice of place than at the hour. He himself spent little time in cafés and when he did so he went just before meals. Moreover it was rather short notice but no doubt there were good reasons for that.

As he packed on Friday he turned on the radio, the English programme since he could follow no other. Normally it was deadly boring but this morning there was an authentic excitement. There'd been another Palestinian outrage, another bombing and an utterly savage one. It had happened in Tiberias where a school bus had been blown to pieces. The dead were already twenty-two and the total was expected to rise. The wounded hadn't been counted yet but children had lost limbs and their sight. Two men had been arrested nearby and were under interrogation.

.... I'm sure.

Charles Russell felt a little sick, not at all in the mood for cups of sweet coffee, but he'd have to keep his new appointment.

The Admiral had arrived before him and rose politely as Charles Russell came in. They sat down to the coffee which Russell had feared and a plate of sweet cakes which he hadn't expected. He thought the Admiral had aged considerably but no doubt he was thinking the same of Russell.

They exchanged the formal courtesies of men who hadn't met for years, then the Admiral said:

'I owe you an apology, Colonel, that I couldn't invite you to come to my home. My wife is expecting a baby, you see.'

'Congratulations.'

'I very much hope so. But I've been warned that it won't be an easy delivery.'

'Doctors are pretty clever nowadays.'

'Doctors,' the Admiral said, 'had better be.' Beyond a husband's natural anxiety was a grimness which Russell found hard to place. Not all births were easy even nowadays, and the Admiral's wife would get first class treatment. The Admiral was holding himself on a rein and Russell doubted the reason was solely his wife.

The Admiral changed the subject clumsily. 'And what do you think of Israel?'

'It's changed.' A platitude no doubt, but true.

'Changed for the better?'

'That's not for me.'

'I think myself that it's changed for the worse.'

The Admiral looked round the café. He was surprised that he couldn't see his shadow and pleased that his absence had saved him the lie that he was really his own and private bodyguard. In any case he wasn't there and he began to talk, relieved to be able to. It was some time since he'd talked to an intelligent foreigner.

'I think we've lost our original spirit.'

'The Arabs might disagree with that.'

'I wasn't thinking of the Arabs, Colonel. I was thinking of our American masters. In practice we're a satellite state.'

This again was too true to be worth denying. The last war had only been narrowly won by an American airlift to save defeat. Russell waited and the Admiral went on.

'I think it's time we went it alone.'

Russell concealed an increasing embarrassment. This wasn't as wild as the really wild men but it was very foolish talk just the same. 'But could you?' he asked.

'We could with oil.'

'Which you haven't got.'

'You misunderstand me, Colonel Russell.' There was the old bite back in the ageing voice. 'I wasn't thinking of oil to sell though that would free us from our shameful subsidies. I was thinking of oil to fight a war.'

'Which the Americans would have to provide if the Arabs were stupid and tried again.'

The Admiral said: 'But if *we* tried again?'

Charles Russell's embarrassment was now something stronger but he couldn't just get up and walk away. This was a man of repute and achievement, and

Russell knew that in the country's capital were men who would back a preventative war. He accepted another round of coffee and nibbled at a cake from politeness. Sweet cakes were not to his taste at any time and in the morning he would rather not see them.

'Oil,' the Admiral said. 'We must have it.'

'Oil for Operation Smash?'

'Where did you pick that phrase up, please?' The Admiral was clearly startled.

'In a newspaper.'

'An Israeli paper?'

'An English one.'

And it might well be done, Charles Russell had thought, to cripple the Arab armies for a decade. The super powers mightn't react with war, too frightened of a confrontation which neither could withdraw from easily. Give a week to those scruffy, superlative soldiers and pan-Arab pretensions might crumble in dust.

Might, might, might and oil, oil, oil. The Admiral had oil on the brain. Charles Russell was decidedly puzzled for no General Staff would risk starting a war if it hadn't the fuel to feed its armour. He said something of this but the Admiral frowned.

'I wish I were sure but I don't see the figures. I'm a has-been, you see, but I'm still an Israeli.'

And an Israeli, Charles Russell reluctantly realized, who might do Israel some final and fatal damage. He would have agreed with Joe Beholden entirely. The Admiral wasn't senile yet, just alarmingly close to the tenuous line where adult judgement fell to pieces.

The Admiral ordered another coffee though Russell had no intention of drinking it. His stomach was awash with coffee; he needed a restorative gin and

Lynne Hammer would have plenty of that. For the moment they were alone in the café.

The bomb had been slid in, not thrown, set to explode from the floor like a tripmine and with much the same and lethal effect. It came to rest against Russell's foot and instinctively he kicked it away. He had heard of men who had thrown bombs back but had never seen it done off the range, and in any case he wasn't thinking but acting on an imperative reflex. So he kicked and dived behind the table. The Admiral was already down and Russell hooked the table over them. He had noticed and admired it already, a fine piece of solid Edwardian craftsmanship. The top was two inches thick, of marble. For a second of time outside all time they waited for the blast in fear.

ELEVEN

Charles Russell woke as he always woke in a single and instantaneous act, one moment in another world, the next with all his faculties working. He was in a comfortable bed and remembered a bang and this conjunction of events had occurred twice before. It was true that this time he felt no pain but that might be only some merciful drug. He began to feel over his body gingerly. His head was in a lightish bandage but when he touched it it didn't do more than ache and there was a plaster on his left ankle. No more.

That established he sat up in bed, looking at his watch on the sidetable. It was eleven o'clock on a sunny morning so they'd sedated him for twenty-four hours. His clearing mind moved up one on its gearbox. . . . Sedated him? Who had sedated him? Presumably doctors, but this certainly wasn't a ward in a hospital. His bed was a luxurious double, something not often found in hospitals. He looked round the room and this too had a message. It was a woman's room but not one for all women. The dressing table bore its load of cosmetics, the side arms which all women found necessary, but they were arranged where the hand would fall on them easily, the most used to the front, the least used at the rear. He tried the bedside light. It worked. It not only worked but threw light for reading. Beyond the bed were the cupboards with sliding doors, one side of glass and the other mahogany. Through the glass he could see the dresses on hangers, arranged with a sort of casual precision.

He nodded; he knew where he was; he rang the bell.

Lynne Hammer came in and wished him good morning. Characteristically he began with apology.

'I'm afraid I'm being a terrible nuisance.'

'Not at all,' she said coolly, 'you were coming here anyway.' It wasn't gracious perhaps but reassuring, the words to put Russell at ease at once. Seeing she'd done so she looked at him, smiling.

'Can you remember what happened?'

'I can.'

'There's a cut on your head — just a matter of stitching it — and a bit which they've taken out of your ankle. Those apart you got away with shock. Lucky that table top was marble. Marble cracks up but it doesn't splinter much. If it did you'd be full of holes as a colander.'

'And the Admiral?'

'I gather he got down first, the old rat, while you were kicking the thing away. So he hasn't got a scratch on him though like you he was pretty badly concussed.' She sat down on the bed and looked at him shrewdly. 'And how is Old Indestructible feeling?' Another woman might have asked that earlier but Lynne Hammer had been a nurse and knew better. She also knew the man in the bed: he'd prefer to have the background first before social questions like 'How do you feel?'

'I'm not too bad,' Charles Russell said.

'Want something to eat?'

'I'd prefer a drink.'

'That's out till the doctor says it's in. But he says you can safely eat if you're hungry.'

'I am a bit.'

'I'll get you some breakfast.'

'If it isn't too much trouble.'

'It isn't.' As she moved to the door he called out to her strongly. 'And tea if you will, please. I'm off coffee for life.'

She returned with an un-Israeli breakfast laid out on a fine old silver tray. She put the tray on the bed while she cleared a table. Her movements were economical, certain.

.... She must have been an excellent nurse.

She watched him silently as he ate his breakfast, then gave him a small cigar and lit it. 'You're sure you don't mind?' He was genuinely touched. Few women would take cigar smoke in bedrooms, they had a compulsion about its fouling the curtains. This one would have them washed or change them but meanwhile he was sitting in bed and smoking. 'What's the prognosis?' he asked.

'For you? Very good if you don't do anything silly. The doctor is coming again this evening and if you ask me he'll keep you in bed a bit longer.'

'Will I be able to walk?'

'In a day or two and without a stick. Meanwhile you can receive a visitor.'

'I didn't know I had one. What's his name?'

'He said he never gave his name and that you'd recognise who he was from that. He added that you'd met before.'

'When is he coming.'

'This afternoon after tea.' Typically she had asked

no questions.

When Beholden's boss arrived at five Lynne Hammer showed him in and slipped away. Russell waved at a chair and the boss sat down. For a moment they looked at each other silently, recognizing less the faces than the disciplined men whom those faces concealed and who had once worked together on common ground. The boss wasted no time on chat or apology.

'Did you read the newspapers yesterday?'

'No. But I gathered from the radio that what happened to us in Dizengoff Street was nothing to what they did in Tiberias.'

'The same people,' Beholden's boss said firmly. 'A sideshow but I'm sure the same people.' He said it without the least change of expression. 'Would you care to hear what we know?'

'Very much.'

'That bombing in Tiberias was done by men who'd escaped from Alidra. Moreover they'd been allowed to escape.'

'How do you work that out?'

'Very simply.' The boss explained in short crisp sentences, subject, verb and object correctly placed. 'There were Palestinian refugees in Alidra and most of them were working in oil. Their leader was a man called el Hakim. They tried for a coup as they did in Jordan but the Sheikh has an army which cut them to pieces. All except twenty-two who were captured. They were put on an island two miles out to sea.' He allowed himself his freezing smile, changing suddenly from statement to question. 'Now how do you rate the practical chances that twenty-two Arabs could all swim two miles?'

'Not very highly.'

'Nor do I. And even if they reached the mainland they'd still need a boat or transport to get away. I conclude as I must they escaped with connivance and connivance at the highest level. In Alidra the highest level means the Sheikh.'

'You believe all twenty-two returned here?'

'I doubt it but we'll soon find out. As you'll have heard we've captured two. They'll talk.'

Charles Russell didn't doubt they'd talk but he'd noticed the other's manner had changed; he was sitting up straighter, his grave face graver. 'But I didn't come here to talk of bombings, much as I regret the fact of them.' He asked the ritual question ritually. 'I may speak to you as a colleague?'

Charles Russell gave the ritual answer. 'At your own and entirely private risk. It's not a habit of mine to break a confidence but that confidence mustn't compromise *me*.'

'That goes without saying. Now listen, please. We're worried about the Admiral. Seriously.'

'The same they tried to get yesterday?'

'Yes.' He said it again without moving a muscle. 'I know you may find it hard to believe but he might bring this state to its knees disastrously.'

'That *is* a little hard to take.'

'I understand that, so here it is.'

He told Russell the story, the whole of the story, since it was pointless to leave him suspecting gaps. He had a favour to ask of a fellow professional and with such you only got favours by truth.

Charles Russell listened in total silence. He didn't waste time in asking questions which experience told

145

him had valid answers. If they hadn't arrested this dangerous Admiral it was because they didn't dare to do so. Russell said at the end of the story simply:

'It does sound a little wild and woolly.'

'Something of an understatement.'

'I didn't mean the plan itself — I suppose that's just conceivably on if everything broke the Admiral's way. I meant the object of the plan — the oil. You've explained to me that a snatch could mean war, and even if it didn't do that you'd have to return the tanker at once.'

'I'd have said the same till yesterday morning.'

'I don't think I follow that.'

'I can't blame you that you don't understand us.' Beholden's boss looked at Russell steadily. 'Politically that oil hasn't changed but emotionally it has changed uncomfortably. I told you it was men from Alidra who murdered our schoolchildren yesterday morning, and no Israeli is going to believe for a moment that they escaped without official help. There'll be a demand for the traditional counterstrike and what better than a shipload of oil? Alidran oil in the port of Eilat would be a very tempting target indeed. No invasion of a foreign territory, no lives at risk, just take that oil. And remember who has brought it in, an established national hero already.' The boss shook his head with a hint of regret. 'Being what we are in Israel I'm delighted that I'm not a Minister.'

Charles Russell had listened to this with sympathy for he recognized a colleague's dilemma, the dedicated high official fearing events and prepared to stand up to them but also fighting the world of politics where decisions must often be made by counting heads. He didn't know his visitor well, he wasn't even sure he much liked him, but he'd worked with him once before successfully and he had never withheld respect where he owed it. Moreover he knew why the boss had called on him, which hadn't been to apologise but to ask for one of two things and maybe both. They were advice and very possibly help. Russell would give the former gladly but doubted that he could serve in the latter. But he could make the situation easier by offering the first advance himself.

'Tell me if I can be of use.'

For the first time that morning the boss relaxed. It was not very much but some tension had gone from him. 'You're extremely kind.'

'We have had the same interests.'

'Then what would you do yourself in my shoes?'

Russell could answer this without thought. 'Nothing dramatic since I gather I couldn't. You used the phrase "a national hero" and that told me all I needed to know. So I think I'd have a word with his wife. I've heard that she's very much younger than he is.' Russell added in his urbanest manner. 'Wives can be very influential and a wife who could be her husband's daughter can often be rather more than that.'

But the boss shook his head. 'We cannot. She's pregnant.'

'So the Admiral told me yesterday. I thought he was making a lot of a commonplace.'

'He wasn't, it's going to be very tricky. In any case we can't approach her. She went into hospital late last night.'

'I had the impression there were other strains on him.'

'Do you wonder with a scheme like that?'

'Why don't you go and talk direct to him?'

'Useless — he'd call my hand at once. He knows perfectly what I can do and what I can't.' Beholden's boss sat up suddenly taut again. The tension which had gone had returned. He asked in a voice which he hadn't used: 'I suppose you wouldn't see him yourself?'

'Whatever for?' Charles Russell was startled and something more for he thought the proposal distinctly cool. . . . First they try to keep me away from the man, then they ask me to pull their chestnuts out. . . . But he said nothing of this to the boss. Instead: 'What makes you think that he'd even listen? There was a relationship once — thirty years ago. Then yesterday we meet in a café. I owe him some coffee and a couple of cakes but I can hardly presume on that to lecture him.'

'We could prepare the way.'

'Whatever for again?' Charles Russell was annoyed but concealed it. He had never been an anti-Semite but was conscious that Jews had certain traits which an Englishman of his type found irritating. For instance an unfeeling persistence, worrying at a bone till they broke their teeth.

As Beholden's boss was doing now. 'You're a man of very great experience. Political experience too.'

'Possibly. But not of this kind. The Middle East was never my stamping ground and in any case we've no language in common. I'm a Gentile and the Admiral isn't. I could talk for a week without making real contact.'

The boss said stubbornly: 'We don't think so.'

'Then I'm sorry that I must still dissent.'

It was polite but it was also final. Beholden's boss

saw it and rose at last. 'Thank you,' he said coolly, 'for listening.'

'Shall we meet again?'

'I very much doubt it.'

In this Beholden's boss was mistaken.

He climbed into his car with a frown for the evening had yielded precisely nothing, but half way back to his office he smiled. It had been a pleasure to deal with another professional, the urbanity cloaking a diamond hard toughness. And toughness in more than one sense — that was evident. He knew that Beholden had once warned Russell that his record showed he was prone to accident and on the history of this visit to Israel he seemed to be exactly that. Russell, the boss had gathered, worshipped no God. That was his own affair entirely but he could hardly deny his guardian angel, and a very efficient angel at that.

The Sheikh had been to a tedious function and at it he'd naturally worn his robes. Now he came back to the modest palace and changed into European clothes. Normally the action was more than physical, since in Arab clothes he thought like an Arab and in a hand-made shirt and well cut trousers he thought like a tolerant European; but he'd noticed that this change of thinking no longer always followed the change of clothes. It was no longer automatic now and sometimes it didn't occur at all, and the Sheikh who'd been taught to look hard at changes had a good idea why this one had happened. He'd been living in an Arab country, Arabs around him for twenty-four hours, an Arab in his bed when he must. He was thinking like one himself and knew it. Nor did this knowledge distress him as once it would.

. . . .That affair of those embarrassing prisoners. Beholden's boss had been perfectly right: he hadn't let them escape, he had laid it on, the boat to the mainland, the lorries afterwards. He'd been tempted to have a couple shot in the interest of making the matter more credible but had decided that he couldn't do it. Kill two, kill the lot, there was little difference, and he'd already decided he couldn't kill all of them. So the Captain of their guard had been summoned, the Commander-in-Chief had been taken aside, the two boatmen had been handsomely feed and the lorries had come from the Sheikh's own transport. Neat, he had thought at the time. Now he didn't.

For he hadn't expected these men would kill again, certainly not an immediate outrage. There were countries where they'd be received as heroes, victims of a reactionary Sheikh whom they'd tried to overthrow but failed. It would have been natural to rest on their laurels a while, but no, they'd gone back to Israel and murdered.

Murdered — it was the only word. The Sheikh had changed but not to that extent. He still had his horror of senseless violence but below it something was stirring yeastily. He would have shied from any word like Arabism but was conscious he was now seeing a case which previously he had shut his eyes to. Many of these so-called refugees had not so much been displaced as displaced themselves. True, but that was a lawyer's statement, the blood in his veins both old and thin. When they came before God for final judgement would the Almighty be harder on half-crazed killers than on those idiots of *Gush Emunim* who'd invented a mythical map of Palestine and insisted that it was theirs exclusively? Murder was worse than trespass, certainly, but organized displacement competed.

He frowned for only months ago he would have dismissed these thoughts as visceral thinking and even now they disturbed his conscious mind. And there were others even more distressing. The State of Israel — what State of Israel? There was rightly a refuge for Jews in Palestine since they'd always been there with many others but today there was something alarmingly different. The Sheikh despised all politicians and they couldn't create a valid State by passing some woolly resolution in an assembly which was itself a bastard. If Israel had title she had it by conquest. Intellectuals thought that wicked: the Sheikh did not. It was a fact which a sensible man must accept and a sensible man would act accordingly.

He was still convinced that his peers had played it wrong. It was stupid to say that war settled nothing: a successful war settled most disputes neatly. But a successful war against Israel was a dream. There was always that secret, deep in the Negev. Perhaps they had it ready and fused or perhaps it was a matter of hours, but the Talion law was a part of their being. Put them anywhere near to a final defeat and Arab capitals would go up in smoke, the mushroom cloud sinking slowly on rubble.

That wasn't the way to settle it. No.

The Sheikh rang a bell to summon a secretary. When in Arab dress he clapped his hands but in European clothes he rang. He told him to bring a file from his private safe.

It had grown in the past few weeks to some size, for the Sheikh had been making discreet inquiries about the land which the man Rifai had coveted and the results had rather more than surprised him. The tract had once been watered and prosperous and that once had not been so long ago. No greybeard could remember it but the greybeards had had grandfathers who had told them they had lived there as children. Four generations — a hundred years. It was nothing in the history of Islam.

The Sheikh turned the pages till he found what he wanted, the report from a team of Swiss geologists. Their cover had been a search for more oil but in fact they had been looking for water and their conclusion had been a long way from pessimism. The watertable had sunk disastrously but water was still there in quantity. It would cost enormous sums to tap it but with modern methods it wasn't impossible.

The Sheikh turned another page and read on. This time it was a Danish agronomist. The soil was in very poor shape indeed, the last stage before irreversible desert, but there it was, still redeemable land. And there was much more of it than Rifai had realized. The Dane had been reluctant to prophesy, certainly not in a formal report, but one day he'd shrugged and chanced it verbally. Given unlimited money from oil, given the water that oil would exchange for, given that there was proper development and no sudden and savage exploitation, this land could support a population and even feed it as it increased inevitably.

Population — that was the awkward word for Rifai had made it sound too easy. No men who had ever borne arms, he had said. Then what men? Ageing, nostalgic fathers of families who would hardly face the initial hardships and were in any case set in the habits of lethargy? The scheme would collapse in a generation. Then ought it to be a final bar that a youth had borne arms in a cause he thought just? The Sheikh's mind was changing and the Sheikh was aware of it. Many of these young men were Marxists and he wouldn't have those since he didn't dare to, and some had committed what he still thought were crimes. But he wouldn't slam the doors of his paradise on a young man who'd picked up a rifle in anger. He'd have done the same himself.

The thought astonished him.

He rang the bell again and said to his secretary: 'Find Mr Rifai and bring him here urgently.'

When Rifai arrived the Sheikh gave him coffee. 'How's the matter of Oceanic progressing?'

'Slowly. But I've got past the front men.'

The Sheikh could well imagine that; he had a high opinion of Rifai's skills or he wouldn't have asked him to play his hand for him. And he could vizualize what was happening perfectly, first the smooth young men with East Coast accents who'd play gentleman-to-gentleman till they saw that that was getting them nowhere. Then they'd withdraw in their Ivy League suits and the real bosses would take their vacant chairs. Rifai had done very well to bring them so fast.

'Have they started to make play with cigars?'

'They light cigars and then don't smoke them.'

'Excellent. And bang the table?'

'They bang the table quite a bit.'

'Make threats to put me out of business?'

'They've done that twice.'

'That's most auspicious.'

'You seem to know a great deal about them.'

'Of course I do, I've met them all. My uncle used me as I'm using you. I had to do it though I hated their bowels. I'd rather face a mob than that lot. A mob can be an ugly thing but those men are a long chalk past mere ugly.'

'I haven't won yet, you know.'

'You're more than half way. You have the advantage that you're not negotiating — no give a foot of this, take an inch of that. I'm proposing to give them nothing whatever and if they shut me down I can still run this country. If they did so a scheme I'm considering seriously would probably have to go to cold storage, but they need my oil more than I need them.'

'What will they do next?'

'Go on bullying. Go on bawling, getting louder.'

'Wish me luck, then.'

'I don't need to. That's the reason I gave you this horrible job.'

'Was there any other reason, sir?'

The question had come very softly indeed but the Sheikh merely smiled in his handsome beard. 'You mustn't be premature, you know.'

When Rifai had gone he smiled again. Rifai was a Palestinian with the gifts he suspected he lacked himself, a talent for large scale innovation and the staying power to wrestle with detail till a great and complex scheme came to fruit. And others of his race would trust him where they wouldn't trust a feudal oil Sheikh. Rifai was as vital to any resettlement as the money from oil which would make it possible.

The Sheikh began to pace his room. He was walking

hand in hand with a dreamer but a dreamer with a worthwhile dream. A dreamer, he thought, with a very rich man. The combination had been known to succeed.

Charles Russell was eating lunch downstairs, the first time he'd done so since coming to Lynne's. It was a good lunch and Lynne was explaining why. 'I can't think why the food in hotels is as horrible as everyone says it is. In a market you can get almost anything — aubergines and sweet potatoes and superlative fruit half hidden by oranges. If you know what to look for the rice is long staple. You can even get very unkosher shell fish if they're certain you're not some Rabbi's spy. The basics are all here for the asking but I suppose the hotels think good food un-American.'

Russell finished his curried prawns in silence, looking round the dining room, trying to pace it. It was certainly not in Lynne Hammer's taste. The furniture was well made and expensive and had come from the best shops in the town, but it was gracelessly copied from other periods, dull and ornate and entirely soulless. The curtains had patterns of nymphs and satyrs. It wasn't Lynne Hammer's room at all.

She saw his look and said with a smile: 'I bought this place from an American actress. I bought it lock stock and barrel — everything in it. As you see, she had pretty doubtful ideas but if I stay I shall bring out some things of my own.'

The conditional surprised him greatly for she'd only been here for a matter of days. He didn't comment directly but said after thought:

'It takes a little time to make friends.'

She made a sound which was measurably close to a snort. 'Friends indeed — friends aren't part of my needs. When I feel like a man I'll find one acceptable and other women mostly bore me. I can play a fair hand of bridge when I have to — the Sheikh was very good at that — but bridge over cups of coffee and biscuits is something I can live without. It isn't friends I need but worthwhile work.'

'I still say you've plenty of time to find it.'

'Maybe, but so far the omens aren't good. I won't do some utterly futile job like sitting in a hotel lobby telling tourists how to find the antiquities, nor did I come here just to be milked. I won't simply sit here spending money, and I've a suspicion that's all they really want of me.'

'You were a nurse,' he said.

'Ah, you're getting closer. I was a nurse and I've got papers to prove it, a pretty good nurse to have got where I did. So naturally I made for a hospital.'

'Don't say they turned you down.'

'Not quite. But I've antennae when I care to use them and they signalled a warning right from the start. So they'll take me all right but they'll never *accept* me. They'll pay me the going rate which is miserable — I can't think how nurses live on it. Presumably, like myself, they find men. But I'll be given all the dirty work and treated like a first year student.'

'You're sure you read the signals right?'

'Listen, Charles, you were always professional. Did you ever have much time for an amateur?'

Again he didn't answer directly. 'But you said you had all the qualifications.'

'It's not what I am but what they think I am. Naturally I didn't tell them that the money wasn't at all important, but I had to give an address and their eyebrows rose. They whispered together — lousy manners — and asked me to wait while they thought it over. So they asked me to wait and the Board went out — a matron, a doctor and some sort of admin man. After five minutes the matron came back. She'd been stuffy at the interview and now she was a whole lot stuffier. They would fix the work permit but would I learn Hebrew? I said I would. As you know, I hadn't intended to do so, but a nurse who can't communicate can't hope to be an efficient nurse. In that case, the old bag said, go and do so. Come back in six months and we'll see if we've vacancies. . . . But couldn't I just go to classes at night and pick up the rest as I worked in a ward? No, I could certainly not do that. It wasn't that they were actively hostile, simply that they had me wrong. They thought I was a comfortable do-gooder who'd be a nuisance in anything like a crisis, and one thing I am not is a do-gooder.'

'Then what are you going to do?'

'Learn some Hebrew. It was a reasonable thing to ask and it's certain I shall get nowhere without it. Meanwhile I'll try at another hospital. They can't all of them be run by morons.'

'May I offer a word of advice?'

'Of course.'

'Next time give a different address.'

She shook her head at once. 'No sir! You don't understand, Charles — for once you don't. I won't take some unpaid work because I'm rich, but nor will I drift into second class jobs on the basis that because

I'm rich I must also be an earnest amateur.'

'Understandable. But it makes things difficult.' He hesitated, then asked her bluntly: 'What'll you do if it breaks the wrong way?'

'I'm afraid I'll have to go home. I'll have failed.'

TWELVE

The Admiral hadn't Charles Russell's resilience and moreover had been bombed twice before. The blast in the Dizengoff café had shaken him and he was secretly ashamed and uneasy that he couldn't throw off the side effects as once he would have done quite easily, the unreasonable irascibility, the sudden flares of frustrated temper when some girl in a shop was stupid or slow. He knew that he was upset and edgy, the last mood in which any worry was welcome.

Nevertheless he sat and worried, for the news from the doctors had not been good. It had been masked in a jargon which was meant to be soothing but the Admiral recognized real anxiety behind the screen of the emollient words. An operation would be inevitable and once it came to the knife one could never be sure. Plenty of men would have reached for the bottle, but alcohol made the Admiral sick and in any case he couldn't be tight when the telephone rang with the final summons.

So he worried till a knock interrupted him. He opened the front door on the Pole. 'We're both of us being watched,' the Pole said. 'There's no point in trying to meet in secret.'

'Why a meeting at all? My wife——'

'I know.' Normally the Pole was subservient but this evening he was making the running. 'I have very important news.'

'Then come in.' The Admiral didn't want to talk politics but there was an urgency in the other's manner which told him that he'd have to do so.

They went up to the Admiral's den and sat down. The Pole said:

'I've been making inquiries.'

'In Alidra?'

'No, inquiries in England.'

'What could interest us in England?'

'Charles Russell. Let me start at the beginning, please.' The Pole was being tiresomely slow. 'I've a brother in England who runs a sweat shop and I asked him to check on Russell. He did so.'

This news only mildly surprised the Admiral since Shin Beth was by no means the only body which regarded every Jew outside Israel as a potential source of information. 'So you checked on Russell. With what result?'

'A very alarming result.'

'Then out with it.' The Admiral was becoming annoyed.

But the Pole held up the broken hand which the Third Reich had left him as shameful legacy. 'You must let me tell the story my way.' Ordinarily he said 'Sir' but now didn't. 'Charles Russell is a friend of the Sheikh. They have apartments in the same block in London and have often met and eaten together. Charles Russell is now in Israel.'

'A tourist.'

'You're perfectly sure he's a tourist? I'm not.'

'And why is that?'

'There's too much coincidence. Now listen to this.

The Sheikh of Alidra had a mistress called Hammer who Russell has also met in London. When the Sheikh returned to Alidra she came to Israel. She now has a rather grand flat in Tel Aviv.' He gave the address; he was being deliberate.

The Pole was being deliberate and the Admiral was losing patience. 'What of it?' It had been a bark.

'Charles Russell has moved to this woman's flat.'

'But you said that he knew her in London.'

'I did.'

The Admiral threw his hands up helplessly. 'Better come to the point before the hospital rings me.'

'The point is that bombing you both escaped from.'

'I was lucky,' the Admiral said, 'but I got down first.' For the first time that evening he managed a smile.

The Pole did not attempt to return it. He suddenly put both fists on the table, a gesture he'd never made before. He said in a voice of stone:

'*Who threw that bomb?*'

'Palestinians, of course. Who else? Remember they'd had two tries already.'

'Would you think so if I also told you that Russell's been talking to Joseph Beholden? He called at his hotel quite openly — I had only to ask to be told. And a good friend has told me something else. When Russell was taken to Mrs Hammer's his first caller was Beholden's boss.'

The Admiral wasn't a slow-witted man and the Pole had always been good at Intelligence. At obtaining it, that is. But at judging it? The Admiral's early impatience had vanished, he was suddenly very attentive indeed.

'Out with it, man. Put it down on the table.'

'Someone has clearly leaked our intention and the Bureau would stick at nothing to stop it. They daren't arrest you, we both know that, so Russell was used to set you up for what would look like a Palestinian outrage.'

'At the cost of his own life?'

'Oh no. There'd be no mention of a bomb, you see; they'd say it was going to bé a shooting. A man would come in and shoot you dead. Russell would be left unharmed.'

'But they did use a bomb.'

'Of course they did.'

'I don't think I follow "Of course".'

It was the Pole's turn to smile and he did so dourly. 'I don't think you ever worked in Intelligence.' This time he added 'Sir' from habit.'

'I know it can be ruthless.'

'It is. Also it likes to minimise risks. If Russell had lived he'd have known the truth and he isn't an Israeli citizen. Once they'd used him they'd like to be sure of his silence.'

The Admiral milled this one over. He was going to have to make an admission and it was one which he would make with shame. 'You've a very good case against the Bureau, humiliating as it is to say it. But I'm less convinced of the case against Russell.'

'Then why did the head of the Bureau call on him?'

'To apologize for the outrage perhaps. They were colleagues in their different fields.'

'Apologies aren't an Intelligence habit.'

'Give me another reason, then.'

'Certainly. He went to warn Russell to keep his mouth shut. As he'd planned it he needn't have given that warning but with Russell still alive he had to. And with it would have gone a hint that what had happened once could happen again.

The Admiral said: 'You have answers to everything.' His voice was at an extreme of bitterness for he was reluctant to think ill of Russell; he said suddenly to the Pole: 'God damn you,' apologizing instantly, shaken at his own unreason. 'In another place at another time bearers of bad news were executed. This is very bad news indeed but I thank you.'

When the Pole had gone he rang the hospital. He'd been told that it was pointless to do so — they'd ring him when there was anything definite — but he couldn't resist the compulsion to telephone.... No, there was nothing yet. They were operating. At this moment the surgeon was shaking his head but this they did not tell the Admiral.

He went back to his vigil, chilled and miserable. What the Pole had told him had genuinely shocked him, but what the Bureau had done was less important than the motive which had made them do it. So his plan had been leaked and that was final. If the Admiral couldn't get down to Eilat the project was dead before it started and there'd be several ways of preventing that, all short of a simple arrest they dare not make. This was the end of the road. He accepted it.

He sighed for the defeat was bitter and the manner of it even bitterer. Only two men had shared his confidence, Ben Arie and the Pole himself. Ben Arie had advised against it and the Pole had merely said it was chancy. As he knew very well himself it was. But that wasn't now the point: the leak was. The Pole would never talk, that was certain; he hadn't even talked as a boy when the Gestapo had maimed his hand for life. Therefore it must be Ben Arie — no other.

The Admiral frowned at a new frustration. A very great wrong demanded atonement and the Admiral knew no way to exact it.

And Russell. In a way that was worse for Russell could have no political motive. However shameful Ben Arie's act Ben Arie was an Israeli citizen. Charles Russell was not, he'd been interfering. And the Admiral had always admired Charles Russell, the sort of Englishman which wasn't now fashionable but which wasn't, in his view, the worse for that. He tried to remember his look and his manner at their meeting in the Dizengoff café. But no, it had seemed entirely normal, he'd been genial and, as always, he'd listened. Either he was an excellent actor or conceivably the Pole was wrong. The Admiral would have liked to believe it, but the Pole knew the ways of that world and he didn't, and he'd had evidence to back his opinion.

He sighed again, alone and wounded.... That damned Charles Russell who he'd believed was a friend. It was another blow, another burden, another in the mounting pressures which had nearly but not yet entirely broken him.

When the telephone rang he ran to it, stumbling. He almost fell but caught at a table. With his other hand he took the receiver. An impersonal voice said:

'Congratulations. You're the father of a healthy boy.'

'And my wife?'

There was a second's silence. 'I think you'd better come round at once.'

164

At the hospital the Admiral mis-parked his car, leaving it on a space marked STAFF ONLY. A matron received him and that was ominous; she gave him a cup of sweet tea; that was worse. She said finally:

'Your son is fine.'

He understood her but he wasn't a coward; he must have it in the words he most feared. 'And my wife?' he asked.

'You must try to be brave.'

He sat for a moment in total blankness, impassive, almost as though he'd not heard her, and the matron watched him in private uncertainty. Delayed shock, she thought, and she didn't like it. This man might go out and do something foolish. Her fellow countrymen were an emotional people and the matron had an authorized therapy. You offered a second cup of tea but this time it wouldn't be only tea. Then you put the man to bed and kept him till the doctor said it was safe to let him go.

'Would you like another cup of tea?'

Again he stayed in his stricken silence and she got up and put a hand on his shoulder. He rose at once. 'No more tea.' He had heard her.

'Then would you like to see the boy?' This was a different drill and sometimes worked.

In this case it didn't. 'Oh no. Not yet.'

'Will you come back tomorrow?'

'Perhaps.'

'We're all of us very sorry indeed.'

There was nothing more the matron could do. She let him go but she did it reluctantly.

He went back to his little car and sat down in it. Another car had been parked to block it and there was a message behind the Admiral's wiper. At first he didn't notice either for he hadn't returned to the workaday world. He wasn't weeping since he was rapt in his vision. . . . Oil — oil after all. Oil should be his parting gift to the woman who had been taken from him. And Charles Russell had shown him the way to reach it, Charles Russell who he'd believed was a friend, Charles Russell who'd joined in a plot to kill him. He owed him no consideration. Charles Russell was now a tool to be used.

When he noticed that his car was blocked he was seized by an unreasoning rage. . . . Some doctor. They had killed his wife. He didn't bother with the windscreen message which in fact told him where to find the car's owner but put his own little Fiat in gear and charged. There was a crash as the bumpers met. Nothing more. The car in front had been locked with its brakes on and in any case was larger and heavier. He backed and charged again, then again. At the third time he couldn't disengage. The two cars were locked together helplessly.

The noise had brought the night porter out but the Admiral ignored his protests. He climbed from the Fiat and started to run, a swaying shambling old man's run, but it took him through the hospital's garden, the porter behind him shouting angrily.

On the road he had to wait for a taxi but he found one and gave the Pole's address. The Pole was in bed and not pleased to be woken but he saw at once that this was a crisis. The Admiral's next words confirmed it.

'Get up at once and bring your gun.'

Like the matron at the hospital the Pole looked at

the Admiral hard, and like the matron at the hospital he wasn't reassured by his manner.

'Where are we going?'

'To Tel Aviv.'

'At this time of night?'

'I've a taxi outside.'

'A taxi?' He was still half asleep.

'Don't ask questions, man. I'll explain in the taxi.' The voice had the bite of authentic authority and instinctively the Pole obeyed it. They went down to the taxi and got in the back. The driver asked the Admiral: 'Where to?'

'To Tel Aviv and make it fast.'

'That'll be three hundred, then.'

'Oh, very well.' He couldn't afford it; he hadn't in fact any money on him. He told the Pole:

'You give the address.'

The Pole blinked twice, he wasn't with it, and the Admiral said with the last of his patience:

'The address you gave me earlier this evening. I don't write everything down, you know.'

The Pole was on to it now and at once uneasy. 'Mrs Hammer's address?'

'Yes, that was the name.'

'Where Colonel Russell is staying?'

'You said so.'

The Pole gave the address and sat back silently. He wasn't a man who frightened easily but now he was running scared and not ashamed.

THIRTEEN

Joe Beholden's boss would be glad to retire but till he did so he meant to stay in control, and control was what he was showing now, a disciplined and icy control which bore no sign of the great effort it cost him. For the taxi driver had gone straight to the police and the police had scented political trouble. Sensibly they had rung the Bureau and the Bureau had brought the boss from his bed who in turn had summoned Beholden peremptorily.

The three of them sat in the boss's room, the boss himself, Joe Beholden, the driver. The driver had told his story well but the boss was recapitulating carefully.

'When he hailed you did you recognize the Admiral?'

'Yes sir. I'd often seen him on telly.'

'Would you say that his manner was normal?'

'No.'

'In what way not normal? Did he seem to be drunk?'

'No, certainly he hadn't been drinking, but he was shaky — all tensed up and trembling.'

'Under great emotional strain?'

'I'd say so.'

'What happened then?'

'He gave me an address to drive to.'

'And there?'

'He went upstairs and came back with another man.

The other man had a pistol.'

'You're sure?'

'I could see it in his trouser belt under his coat.'

'Then you drove them to Tel Aviv. Did they talk?'

'They talked to each other but not to me.'

'Can you tell us what they said?'

'I didn't understand their language but I know that it wasn't English or German.'

'What was your impression?'

'Sir?'

'I mean what sort of conversation was it? An argument, for instance?'

The taxi driver considered this. 'Come to think of it, it probably was. The Admiral was doing most of the talking and the other man seemed to be disagreeing.'

'Strongly?'

'Yes, at times very strongly.'

'Then when you'd got to the second address they'd given you, the one in Tel Aviv, what happened?'

'They got out and I asked for my fare but I didn't get it.'

'What did you do?'

'What could I do? I knew the other man had a gun.'

'You're sure about the address?'

'Quite sure.'

'You saw them go in?'

'No, not actually in. It's a block of apartments and they went to the portal. One of them rang the bell. I drove back.'

'And went straight to the police?'

'I was owed three hundred.'

'You did well,' the boss said. 'I'll see you're looked after.'

He dismissed the driver and sat in silence. Presently he said to Beholden:

'It's ironical if you look at it one way. We've been falling over our clumsy feet to prevent Charles Russell meeting the Admiral and now the same Admiral snatches Russell.'

'Snatches him?'

'Holds him as hostage.' The boss produced his wintriest smile. 'Locally it's the classic method. It would come to the Admiral perfectly naturally since it is something which is done here most weeks. And we're entitled to remember too what the Admiral was before he became one. Working in IZL was pretty tough.'

'Hostage,' Beholden said, 'then demand.' He hesitated. 'What sort of demand?'

'He can't be quite so unbalanced yet as to suppose we'd give him active help so the demand is almost certainly negative. Take your men away and get off my back. Don't try to stop me reaching Eilat.'

'Demand to be met or the hostage has had it.'

'Our policy is to let that happen or alternatively to shoot it out. But in this case we do not dare do either. This isn't a snatch by foreign terrorists. The Admiral is an Israeli citizen, one with a public reputation, and Russell is an eminent Englishman whose death by violence would not pass unnoticed. Our normal weapons are not available so we'll have to go down to that flat and talk.'

'Suppose they're on the road already.'

'Then we're in very serious trouble indeed and I'll do whatever I can to forstall it. But I think there's a chance that they're still at that flat. Remember this can't have been planned — it's impromptu. They

170

haven't got a car for instance, and though Mrs Hammer probably has I doubt if it's kept in the street outside. They'll have to feel their way as they go and Russell is clever and won't make it easy even with a gun in his back. I think there's a hope we can catch them before they move.'

'How do we play it then, sir?'

'By ear.'

Beholden's boss had been clearing his mind but now his voice changed into firm sharp orders. 'We'll go separately and meet at the door. On your way you're to pick up Ben Arie and bring him.'

'Ben Arie? What for?'

'You'll find that out later.'

'Suppose he has a woman with him.' Beholden knew Ben Arie's habits.

'You needn't bring the woman too.' The boss had delivered it beautifully deadpan.

'Then suppose he won't come.'

'You may use force to bring him.'

'He's a member of the Knesset.'

'I know.'

Beholden swallowed twice but said: 'Right.'

The boss looked at his watch. 'Say eighty minutes. Fifty to Tel Aviv for both of us and the half an hour extra for collecting Ben Arie.'

He used his own half hour on the telephone. . . . They might get hold of a car by theft or menace so another was to be ready to follow. No, do not intercept, just follow. So a watch on the Hammer flat immediately and reports of any events by radio. Airports to be alerted at once, especially the one in north Tel Aviv which handled the light aircraft traffic. And put a block on the Eilat road forthwith. . . . No again, do *not* arrest. Take the Admiral to the nearest police station on some query about a traffic offence and hold him till I arrive myself. If they get that far there'll be another man with them, possibly a woman as well. Extend the utmost courtesy to both.

The boss looked at the time again; he had ten minutes to spare. He was a religious man and he spent them in prayer. Then he called his own car and drove to Lynne Hammer's.

On the way the radio broke his thoughts. It was the watch on Lynne Hammer's flat in position. There were lights inside and occasional movement. Nobody had been seen to leave.

'Are you awake, Charles?'

He said he was. He didn't add the ungracious word 'now' for she wasn't one to wake a man on some idle whim which would keep till the morning. If she wanted to talk it was something serious.

'I've been to two other hospitals and both of them turned me down again.'

'Tell me. It may help a bit.'

He got up and made a pot of tea. He doubted that he'd sleep again but he could recognize real distress when he heard it. He gave her the tea and she thanked him gratefully. 'You're a very tolerant man.'

'I'm an ear.'

'So it went like this or something like it. The first hospital wasn't so bad — less stuffy. They wanted qualified nurses badly and they didn't go on about not speaking Hebrew. Naturally I would have to learn it but how I did that was my private business. In any case I'd have had to have some if I was going to apply for Israeli citizenship. When I said that I didn't intend to it shook them. . . . So I'd come to Israel and wanted to work there but I wasn't prepared to become an Israeli? I said that was correct but not why. Nor did they press me — they simply lost interest. They were all or nothing people, not like me. Not, now I come to think of it, like anything I could have worked with happily.'

'So in one way you had a lucky escape.'

'Cold comfort, Charles. I was still without work.'

'Then what happened at the second place?'

'That was straightforward humiliation. We got along fine at first and I thought I was in. Then they started on the personal questions and you know what I feel about not pretending. Was I a widow? No, divorced (I was married for six months, you know, and Hammer was the big brute's name). Was that recently? No, it was years ago. Then they looked at a form which I'd filled in first. But I hadn't been nursing for quite some time? No, I hadn't been nursing for quite some time. And I was living at the address as shown? I could see what they were thinking all right. They were thinking I was a high-class tart, getting a little past it perhaps, and anxious for a steady job. Then they began to press me hard. I didn't like it but I wanted that job. Had I money of my own? Yes, I had. A man friend? Yes. That finished it. They didn't physically throw me out but I could see they were itching to do just that.'

He was thinking that she'd been less than tactful but he knew that all pretences offended her. He said at length:

'I respect your integrity.'

'A fat lot of good it's done me, hasn't it?'

'Oddly enough I think it has. If they won't accept you for what you are it's better they shouldn't accept you at all.'

'I think so too when I think of it calmly. At this moment I'm not thinking calmly. I want real work and I'm not going to get it here. I'm not going to be some businessman's hack and I'm not going to play at social service. They don't want me as I am. So be it. I'll go back to England, defeated, and try again.'

'You could give it another whirl,' he said. But he didn't believe the result would be different.

'No sir,' she said. 'I know when I'm licked.'

He had an instinct she would have been grateful for tears but he'd never even imagined her weeping. She got out of the warm bed slowly.

'I'll make another pot of tea.'

Beholden's orders had been to bring Ben Arie. They'd been totally incomprehensible but the boss had been in no mood to explain and in any case there hadn't been time. He took a car and a driver but not a gun. He wouldn't need a gun with Ben Arie and the boss had made it clear in terms that whatever came later in Tel Aviv it wouldn't be an old-fashioned shoot-out. That wasn't his business: Ben Arie was.

Ben Arie had a two-roomed apartment in an ageing block without a porter and Beholden inspected the lock with a smile. It should take him three minutes at most.

It took two.

There was a light on in the bedroom still and Beholden turned the knob and went in. Ben Arie, as he'd supposed, was not alone. Beholden said politely:

'Good morning.'

'What's the meaning of this?' Ben Arie was furious.

'I have orders to take you to Tel Aviv.'

'Preposterous'. His colour was rising.

'Nevertheless those are my orders.' The girl had started to get out of bed.

'I'll have you broken for this.' He was blustering now.

Beholden walked to the head of the bed where Ben Arie was sitting up and frothing. He was tempted to use rather more than persuasion for he knew how to hurt without seriously maiming and he loathed Ben Arie and all his works. But discipline and training held. He'd been told he might use force if necessary but the necessity was not yet established. The girl had begun to dress and he turned to her.

'You are perfectly free to go.'

She was silent but Ben Arie was not. 'Go straight to the police,' he told her. 'At once.'

She stared at him in surprise, then laughed. There was mockery in the sound and contempt. She wasn't the sort to go near the police. She finished dressing and turned to Beholden.

'Thank you,' she said.

'For nothing. Good luck.'

When she had gone Beholden spoke again. 'You see?' he said.

Ben Arie saw. He got up too and began to dress.

Russell hadn't expected to sleep again but in fact had dropped off when the door phone woke him. It was going to be one of those nights, he thought, as he went into the hall to answer it. If the sound had woken Lynne she hadn't moved.

He picked up the receiver to answer it. It was probably some drunk or the police for Lynne sometimes left her car where she shouldn't. 'Yes?' he said irritably, 'Yes, what is it?' He wasn't going to press the release till he knew rather more of whoever had woken him. He hadn't looked at his watch since he didn't need to. The private clock of his own metabolism had told him it was just before dawn.

A known voice answered and gave its name. 'Colonel, you're in very great danger.'

'But Admiral——'

'We must talk at once.'

Russell hesitated for quite a time. He thought the Admiral was a man under pressure and had told Joe Beholden's boss that he did so, but he hadn't considered him irresponsible and they had shared a very positive danger. It was a strange and in some ways a savage country and there was a woman asleep in bed upstairs. He decided to temporise.

'Please to wait.'

He went back to the bedroom, put on shoes and a dressing gown. Lynne Hammer was still breathing evenly — he had seen her take two pills with the second tea. He went downstairs and pressed a switch, for the light on the portal was controlled from inside. Then he looked through the spyhole: two men were standing there. Indubitably one was the Admiral but the other he had never seen. There was no car in the street behind them and that was strange.

He opened the door on the chain. 'Good morning.'

'Please let us in. We're in danger too.'

'What sort of danger?'

'Damn it, isn't once enough?'

Whether by luck or perhaps by judgement the Admiral had chosen the perfect words. Once *had* been enough, rather more than enough, and with a woman to consider too three men would be very much better than one.

He took the chain off, pulling the door wide open, and the second man put a gun in his stomach.

FOURTEEN

The boss told his driver he needn't press it since it was pointless to arrive at Lynne Hammer's before Beholden had collected Ben Arie. Ben Arie was the key, the essential. Without him they hadn't a hope in hell.

Beholden's boss smiled: it had come to him suddenly. He had spent his youth in Germany and kept a German mistrust of inspiration, so as he drove to Tel Aviv in the small hours he applied his powerful and lucid mind to probing for earthly but fatal holes in a plan which he was convinced was heaven-born.

For the life of him he couldn't see any. He had stated the limitations already when talking to Beholden earlier: there was a barbarous game called Hijacks and Hostages but Israel refused to accept its rules. Hostages were never ransomed nor any demand in their name conceded. An attempt would be made to rescue them and one or two such had been hugely successful, but where that wasn't possible or where it had been tried and failed the hostage was written off as a casualty in a war which Israel had not declared.

The boss accepted this policy loyally but in this case it was alas inapplicable. The Admiral had gone to Lynne Hammer's flat and taken with him a man with a gun. In that flat were Mrs Hammer and Russell so he'd be holding them against some demand. What demand? That couldn't be predicted with certainty since the Admiral had, by hypothesis, broken, but a very good guess stood out a mile: he'd demand unhindered travel south and a day or two in the port of Eilat free from surveillance of any kind and free to achieve his end if he could. To concede that demand was of course impossible, but to refuse it invoked the grim alternatives and neither was in this case tempting. The boss knew all about the Pole. He wasn't some neurotic Arab but had proved himself in the hardest school, the school of a callous and ruthless Gestapo. If the Admiral told him to kill he would, and neither Russell nor Mrs Hammer herself were mere names on a list of unfortunate travellers. Charles Russell was a well-known Englishman and Mrs Hammer was still an American citizen. The former's death by a PLO bomb in a café would have been something to be regretted publicly but his murder at an Israeli's hands would be a matter far less easily slid from. As for Mrs Hammer, who knew? She might have been a President's mistress. So calling the bluff wasn't on. Not in this case.

Nor was the alternative, which was to go in with guns and shoot it out. The Pole might be expendable but the Admiral very certainly wasn't. He was a highly respected Israeli citizen and his death by shooting would raise an uproar. If that shooting had been done by the Bureau that uproar might sweep away a government. So shooting was out too.

But it wasn't. It had come to him in a blinding flash. *It all depended who did the shooting.*

He had stood at once to give heaven his thanks, convinced that no other source was conceivable. The plan had the classic grace of simplicity. . . . Take Ben Arie with you and blow him wide to the Admiral, tell him he'd been your man all along, not the trusted adviser the Admiral thought him. The Admiral wouldn't pass that at any time and now that he was at best disturbed, at worst as mad as a man could be, there was an excellent chance he'd react with violence.

When Ben Arie would be deservedly dead but the Admiral wouldn't go to prison. Good gracious no, not our fine old Admiral. Our fine but alas not quite normal Admiral. Psychologists would appear by the dozen, from Manhattan across Europe to Tilsit, swearing in their preposterous jargon that the Admiral wasn't fit to plead. He'd be put away quietly and die in comfort. Beholden's boss wished that fate upon no man, particularly not on one he respected, but it was better than facing a screaming scandal and much better than an unwanted war.

His driver saw his smile and asked him:

'Care to share the joke, sir?'

'I can't.' The boss shut him up but not unkindly. 'You could call it a state secret,' he said, 'if you were ass enough to talk in platitudes.'

The gun was now in Charles Russell's back as he preceded the man who held it up the stairs. He was angry and humiliated but he wasn't, at this moment, frightened. As likely as not that would come quite soon but he'd been at gunpoint before and survived the experience. No doubt that proved nothing beyond good fortune but luck had a habit of running to form. He had left the door of the flat wide open and as they reached the landing the Admiral spoke.

'Where's the living room, please?'

Charles Russell noticed the 'please' and approved it. The Admiral might be disturbed or worse but his manners hadn't cracked with his mind. 'Straight in and second right.'

'Many thanks.'

They went in and sat down and Charles Russell waited. The Admiral said something in Hebrew and the Pole put the pistol away in his trouser belt. 'Where is Mrs Hammer, Colonel?'

'Mrs Hammer is in bed asleep.'

'We do not have any need of her but it would be unfortunate if she did anything foolish.'

'If it interests you she has taken two sleeping pills.'

The Admiral said he understood but Russell was very certain he didn't. He would know she was American and had assumed she could only sleep on some drug. In fact she slept as he did, excellently, and only took a very mild sedative when some rare emotional crisis demanded it.

The Admiral appeared to be thinking this over but in fact he was thinking of something else. Charles Russell must be told his intention but must he also be told the justification, that he believed that Russell had worked with the Bureau in what would look like a Palestinian killing and was therefore fair game to the friend he'd betrayed? He decided that he wouldn't do so. Russell would deny it hotly, there could even be an altercation, and a dispute wouldn't bring him a mile nearer Eilat. He made this decision quickly then spoke.

'You will have realized that you're a hostage.'

'I'd guessed it. May I ask to what end?'

The Admiral told him.

Charles Russell sat in a total silence. The plan was mad but the word impermissible, for the cliché about Israeli Spectaculars was one with an irrefutable basis. . . . An Arab air force destroyed like ducks caught on water, and no other people could have pulled off Entebbe. True, the Germans had achieved a pale copy, that had been done with the active help of a state on whose soil an aircraft had landed, defying repeated orders not to. Or Milestone One Hundred and One. Unbelievable. The road to Cairo undefended and an Egyptian army trapped in Sinai. It had needed the awful might of America to prevent a debacle and maybe world war. 'Impossible', Charles Russell decided, was not a word to use in Israel. 'Mad' would be even more foolish and dangerous. So he kept his peace and the Admiral went on.

'Mrs Hammer has a car no doubt.'

'Mrs Hammer has indeed a car.'

'Where does she keep it?'

'I assume in her garage.'

'Where is her garage?'

'Below this flat.'

'Where are the keys?'

'I don't know.'

'Then ask her.'

'Mrs Hammer, as I told you, is sleeping.' Charles Russell wasn't being heroic, simply playing for time which he sensed was his friend. And he had noticed something he thought important. The Admiral might be mad as a hare but like many men of his type and background the prospect of action had steadied him notably. He was incapable still of proper judgement but his manner was creeping close to normal.

'We've got to have a car, you know.'

'Then perhaps you should have planned more carefully.'

'No doubt you are right.' The Admiral was now collected, the formidable field commander. 'I think I can read your mind, my friend. It tells you that we could easily kill you but if we did so we'd have no weapon left.' This was uncomfortably close to the truth and Russell was too wise to comment. 'But what I think you underrate is the power of what is called persuasion. We don't have to kill you to get those keys'. He snapped something to the Pole, who stood up. Russell stood too. This would all consume time. As he did so he could see from the window. The dawn was still struggling in the pangs of its birth but the street lights were flaring and Russell saw clearly. He said to the Admiral:

'Look from the window.'

'There is something of interest?'

'I believe you will think so.'

'No tricks, mind.'

'What tricks? Your friend has a gun and I have not.'

The Admiral went to the window and opened it. Four men were in a car outside the flat. One had binoculars and was watching the Admiral, another was talking into his radio. The two in the back had their hands in their laps. The Admiral couldn't see what they held but he considered it an easy guess.

He returned from the window: they all sat down.

'You are perfectly right. My planning was extremely slipshod and the fact it was made under pressure no excuse. I've been followed for some time, you see, and those men outside will be men from the Bureau.'

Russell started to speak but the Admiral silenced him; he was talking almost impersonally now, making a fresh appreciation. 'But as it's broken I think it's broken my way. The original plan was distinctly crude — to drive down to Eilat with you at gunpoint, bluffing our way through attempts to halt us. Now we can talk to the Bureau directly and fix it without leaving this room.'

'Those men outside don't look like fixers.'

'Exactly. May I use the telephone?'

Russell nodded and the Admiral did so. There was a brief exchange in quickfire Hebrew, then the Admiral returned with a smile.

'They're already on their way — the boss himself. This is really going to be very interesting.'

'Interesting perhaps, but fruitless.'

'You don't think my hand is good enough?'

'No. And in any case you've got it wrong — I mean the oil which you intend to pirate. It won't be the gift to your country you think it. Instead it will be a poisoned chalice.'

'I disagree but tell me why.' The need for action had calmed him already, and between bouts of action he'd never fretted. He wasn't fretting now but listening, not frittering his strength in impatience. He was not only willing to listen to Russell; he was actively anxious to hear his opinion.

Which Russell was giving, watching the Admiral. He would have to get his manner just right. Any undertone of misunderstanding, a hint he didn't feel an Israeli's passion, would probably make the Admiral angry and anger was his most evident enemy. The pendulum of his mind was swinging but it hadn't yet settled on solid sanity. Charles Russell would have to be very careful; he must be rational but not overly logical, authoritative but without pomposity; he said at length:

'I think you've got the balance wrong. A shipload of crude is a worth while prize but it isn't going to last for ever.'

The Admiral conceded it. 'Perfectly true.'

'No Arab state will sell you a bucketful, so when Kissinger took away Abu Rhodeis he made a little arrangement with Persia. You would give up what you'd taken from Egypt and Kissinger would fix the Shah. By and large he seems to have kept his promise, but infuriating the Americans, as seizing a cargo of oil would do, is a very dangerous game indeed.'

The Admiral began: 'We have friends in America——' but Russell cut him short though politely.

'And very powerful friends they are. But this isn't an election year and there's something else I would think more ominous.'

'Tell me,' the Admiral said.

'I mean to. Your friends, as you say, are influential. It would be hard enough to lean on Israel, unthinkable to do so publicly. But a word in a Persian ear would be private and the consequences immediately fatal.'

The Admiral thought it over deliberately. 'You have a lucid mind which I greatly envy. Unhappily you're not an Israeli.' He rose and walked to the window again, saying as he turned his back to the room: 'They're taking their time about getting here, aren't they?' There was a hint of impatience now but not febrile.

Charles Russell said: 'Would you like some coffee?'

'Can I trust you to make it?'

'You needn't chance it.' It was a woman's voice and the three men turned to her. Lynne Hammer was in slacks and a sweater. Her hair was tied up but her make-up scrupulous. 'I've been shamelessly listening in,' she said. 'Deplorable but it saves explanations. Now I'll make you that coffee.'

She went to do so.

She returned with the coffee and tea for Russell, pouring them and sitting down. 'What I cannot understand,' she said coolly, 'is the real reason why you want that oil. I heard what you said to Charles and he to you. Very logical it all was — convincing. But I'm a woman and it didn't convince me. There's something behind all this.'

'There is.' The Admiral had taken ten seconds to say it but when he did so he spoke with a casual ease which up to that moment he hadn't come near to. Something had passed between them, Russell saw. Not sex or at least not immediate sex but something more permanent. Understanding.

'Tell me,' she said.

'Oil would have been my final present to a woman I very dearly loved.'

'Final?' It was almost inaudible.

'My wife died in childbirth early this morning.'

'I'm very sorry indeed to hear it.' A hesitation, then it came determinedly. 'And the baby?'

'A boy.'

'Alive and well?'

'I'm told so. I haven't seen him myself.'

'You *what*?' Lynne Hammer didn't believe what she

186

heard. 'You mean you drove down here on this crazy scheme without looking at the son she'd given you?'

'I'm afraid I did,' the Admiral said. For the first time he sounded apologetic.

'You thought of oil as a final present. Wouldn't caring for her son be a better one?'

'How can I care for a baby alone?'

'Admiral,' she said at last, 'Admiral, Excellency, whatever they call you. Admiral, you're a very great coward.'

He flushed but he didn't deny it directly. 'I was under increasing pressure,' he said.

'I can understand that but not where it led you.' She lit a cigarette and inhaled it, then blew two strong streams through her nose like a man. The gesture was unfeminine but something very female was happening. Russell sensed it and wisely held his tongue. The Pole who knew no English did the same. Physically they were both still present, but physical presence apart they had ceased to exist. Lynne said at length:

'So what are you going to do?'

'I don't know.'

'You can't leave him in a hospital nor send him to some soulless orphanage.'

'I thought that perhaps my first wife's relations——'

'No.' She had almost but not quite barked it.

'I don't think you understand how I'm placed. I'm alone and I'm not at all well off. I can't afford a nurse or a housekeeper.'

'I'm an excellent nurse and have papers to prove it.'

'I imagine your fees would be rather high.' He was looking round the room as he said it.

'My fees would be precisely nothing.'

'I couldn't accept your charity.'

'Rightly. But there wouldn't be any question of charity.'

'I don't think I follow.'

Lynne sighed wordlessly and Charles Russell smiled. She was thinking about men. They were slow.

'I am offering you marriage, sir.'

In the silence which followed he watched the Admiral. He was a man of a different race and he couldn't read him. But it was possible the Admiral was reading Lynne Hammer. As the Sheikh had once remarked to Rifai she didn't look like a Jewess; she didn't think like one. But he remembered a commando raid, two men with their faces blacked up like coons. They'd never met before in their lives but without a word spoken they'd teamed together. He'd been impressed at the time and now he was fascinated. Recognition signals, that New but in practice ageless Biology. . . .

The Admiral looked round the room again, 'Madam, I take it you're not very orthodox.'

'I'm not orthodox at all,' she said. It was an understatement but not precisely a lie.

'Nor am I but there's another obstacle.'

'I can't see any obstacle.'

'I can. You are evidently rich. I am not.'

'You've a pension to pay for your personal comforts and you're offering me a reason to stay here. On balance I'd say I owed you money.'

He thought for some time, then stood up formally; he bowed gravely and he didn't smile.

'Madam, I accept your offer.'

'Thank you. Then I'll make you all breakfast.'

The boss told his driver to stop the car. Joe Beholden's had already arrived and the boss got down and walked across to it. Ben Arie was in the back looking frightened but for the moment the boss had no use for Ben Arie. He'd decided that he must first play it formally, using reason as an outside chance. If that failed, as he expected it would, he would bring in Ben Arie and play it that way. He asked Beholden:

'They're still inside?'

Joe Beholden jerked a thumb, confirming it.

'Then wait here for exactly ten minutes. If I'm not out in that time come in with Ben Arie. If you hear shooting come in at once.'

'Would you like the driver's gun, sir?'

'Certainly not.'

Beholden's boss rang the bell and waited, astonished when Charles Russell opened. 'Good morning,' he said, 'we were rather expecting you.' He held the door wide open politely. 'We're all having breakfast. Please come in.' He led the way to the dining room. 'I don't think you've properly met Mrs Hammer but everyone else I'm sure you know well.'

Lynne Hammer said: 'Would you like some breakfast?'

The boss hesitated. 'I'd be grateful for coffee.' Russell waved at a chair. 'Then please sit down.'

The boss sat down and drank his coffee. He was totally at a loss and he wasn't often; he'd come prepared for mayhem or murder but not for a domestic meal. Charles Russell concealed his amusement and watched him. The Admiral was eating a hearty breakfast and Russell was watching that breakfast too. Lynne had been giving him English breakfasts but this morning it was rather different. Besides the inevitable scrambled eggs, there was some faintly repellent cold fish and cucumbers, cheeses and something sweet in a bowl, half way between a jam and a puree. Russell hadn't even known she had them. When the boss had finished his coffee he looked at Lynne.

'You will excuse us a minute?'

'Of course.'

Russell took the boss to the comfortable sitting room and lighted his after breakfast cigar. 'You would like me to start?'

'I would indeed.'

'The Admiral has abandoned his plan.'

'How do you know?'

Charles Russell told him. 'So you see,' he concluded, 'she's switched him neatly. He has a one-track mind like all great commanders and for the moment all he cares for or thinks of is the welfare of his late wife's child. After all, that's a very much better present than a shipload of highly embarrassing oil.'

Beholden's boss didn't answer at once. 'I agree it's clever but will it hold?'

'I think it will. There's another factor.'

The boss raised his eyebrows and Russell answered them. 'Your Admiral may not be young any more but I'd guess he was still attractive to women. There are even women who like them older.'

'You should know that,' the boss said acidly.

'I think that's distinctly unkind. Also envious. In any case we'd do well not to quarrel.'

'You're perfectly right. I beg your pardon.'

'Then you'll give it a chance?'

'I reserve my position.'

Charles Russell had heard the phrase before and it was one which he despised and detested. It meant, when you stripped it down to bare meaning, that the speaker hadn't made up his mind. 'Don't reserve it too long.'

'Why not?'

'You can't.'

'Who says I can't?'

'I'm afraid that I do.'

The boss started to rise but sat down again quietly. This Russell had been perfectly right: they'd get nowhere if they started to bicker. 'Put your hand down,' he said.

'I intend to do so. You remember that affair in the café? Now suppose it wasn't Palestinians. Suppose it was you trying to kill the Admiral. And incidentally my inconvenient self.'

'Nonsense,' Beholden's boss said promptly.

'Nonsense it very probably is. I can't even say that I really believe it.'

'In any case you can't prove such rubbish.'

'Precisely the point. I don't need to prove it.'

'That doesn't make sense.'

'Then here it comes. You once sent Beholden to London to head me off. When I got here you read me a tedious lecture about somebody called Colonel Charles Russell — how he could never escape his background, all the rest. It bored me so I'm throwing it back at you. If you believe all that I could still make things difficult.'

'Put it in terms, please.'

'That's perfectly fair. So if I breathed into certain receptive ears that I'd come to Israel, an innocent tourist, and that the Bureau had tried to shorten my life I shouldn't be asked for proof or evidence. The shutters would simply come down with a bang. You wouldn't get further cooperation and with things as they are you're needing it badly.'

The boss said surprisingly mildly: 'That's blackmail.'

'Not a word to use to a fellow professional.'

The boss very seldom laughed but now he did. When he had recovered he said:

'Let us compromise. I will give her six months to hold him if she can. If she succeeds that ends the matter, but if she does not I must think again.'

'Reasonable,' Russell said. 'And agreed.' Privately he thought six months generous. In six months she would have him feeding from hand. 'More coffee?' he suggested blandly.

They went back into the dining room. The others had finished but the Pole was still eating. There was coffee still and fresh tea for Russell. Beholden's boss stared at it, polite but incredulous.

'You really prefer it?'

'For the moment I'm distinctly off coffee.'

'I think you do very well to choose tea. Tea seems to suit the English genius.'

He didn't define the word but Russell smiled.

FIFTEEN

'And so,' the Sheikh said, 'Oceanic has backed down.'

'Just as you said, sir. They've simply gone home.' Rifai wasn't hiding his satisfaction.

'With nothing to show for attempted blackmail?'

'Nothing.'

'Then you'll have to think of a title.'

'A what?'

'Designation would be a better word. For the new job which I'm going to give you.' He smiled but Rifai did not return it. 'Minister of Development? Corny. Minister of the New Lands? Worse. Think up one yourself in your leisure time.'

'I shan't have a lot of it.'

'No, you won't. But you'll have almost everything else you need — money which I know you'll use wisely and my personal and political backing if political backing is ever necessary. In this sort of state it probably won't be. Of course you can't use Israeli technicians, which I believe was your original plan when you were dependent on Israeli help to get me where you wanted me, on a string. Nor do you need them. A Swiss and a Dane have been doing some fieldwork and there are men who make this sort of work their lives. Pick good ones and pay them well. They will serve us.'

'It's all going to take some time.'

'It is. And I know what you're thinking and so am I.

You're thinking that events may outrun us. There could easily be another war and it's conceivable, just barely conceivable, that this time we'd come out as winners. That's a question which won't be decided here but in a country with a different culture. There aren't many Jews in the State of Georgia and I sense that the Great American People is getting a little tired of that lobby. So if Israel went down new lands would be purposeless. You Palestinians would come flooding back to what you mostly mistakenly call your homelands and what we are trying to do would be pointless. Nevertheless I'm accepting the gamble.' They rose and embraced. 'Please start at once.'

When Rifai had gone the Sheikh sat down again. In one way he was feeling elated for a worthwhile dream was approaching reality, but in another he felt flat and frustrated. He'd been seeing a lot of Rifai, but who else? In his position friends were too dangerous even if he'd much liked his own people. He thought of Lynne Hammer with sharp regret. She had written once and he hadn't answered. Naturally she hadn't written again. Why should she? She was committed now.

So for that matter was he himself. He'd been born to it and could never escape it.

He sighed and went about his duties.

The boss had two engagements that morning and both of them would be giving him pleasure. He'd come back to his office the previous day and had used what had been left of it to reassess the new position, to tidy up an end or two which events had left unexpectedly dangling.

The first of these was to deal with the Pole but the boss saw no great trouble in that. There was a file on the Pole and the boss had reread it. On the whole it had reassured him comfortably for the Pole had always kept his covenants. He sent for him and sat him down, looking at his stolid face but sensing the unconscious dignity which simple men so often exuded. He'd decided he wouldn't play tricks with the Pole but exchange understandings and stick by his own.

'You realize you've been extremely foolish.'

The Pole didn't answer and none was expected.

'If the Admiral had embarked on his plan you'd have both of you been in serious trouble. Jail at the best and maybe worse.'

'I've known worse than jail,' the Pole said quietly. He had looked at his mangled hand as he said it.

'What are you going to do now?'

'What can I?'

'You could, for instance, keep your mouth shut, say nothing of recent events whatever.'

'Is that a request or an order?'

'Neither. I am making you a proposition. What were you doing before you went in with the Admiral?' It was a question though the boss knew the answer.

'I was a bricklayer till the building boom burst.'

'Would you like to work again?'

'Of course.'

'Then I'll arrange for you to start tomorrow but the moment you open your trap you're out. And turn in that silly pistol.'

'Done.'

They shook hands on it with a solemn formality.

Beholden's boss sat down to think again for the next

visitor would be Ben Arie and Ben Arie, if things had gone to plan, would be dead as he richly deserved to be. Alive he would have to be handled firmly. As Russell, the boss thought dourly, handled me. Russell hadn't in fact had a crushing hand but he'd played it with a cool urbanity which had made it look like four aces plus. The boss didn't feel he could quite match Russell but at least he had learnt a lesson. He'd use it.

So he let Ben Arie begin indignantly. 'I've come here because you insisted.'

'Quite so.' It was spoken with a quiet acidity which told more of their respective positions than any amount of explanation.

'But I don't understand what game you're playing. I was taken from my bed by night, then driven to Tel Aviv and brought back again. I think you owe me an explanation.'

'No explanation whatsoever.'

Ben Arie flushed. 'I was pulled from my bed by force——'

'Try to prove it.'

'As it happens I can. That girl——'

'You know her name?'

'Of course I do.' But he sounded uncertain. Come to think of it he knew a name but that didn't establish she always used that one.

'As a witness such a woman is useless. The police know her well and found her easily. Since she can only live with a certain police tolerance she will swear to whatever the police suggest to her. Which will not include the word duress.'

Ben Arie changed from indignation to a bluster which the boss despised. 'I'll break you for this.'

'I very much doubt it. On the contrary I am breaking you.' The boss began to dish it out; he loathed Ben Arie and now he had him. 'If it wasn't force which took you there why did you go to Tel Aviv?'

Ben Arie wasn't slow; he stayed silent.

'You went to an American's flat where Russell was holed up with the Admiral. The Admiral had a man with a gun.' The voice changed into an unkind parody of a bullying counsel in a rather weak court. 'I suggest that you knew the Admiral's plan.'

'Of course I did and I passed it on to you.'

'Dangerous, wasn't it?'

'Very dangerous.'

'Then why drive to Tel Aviv in the small hours if it wasn't to cooperate?'

'You know the reason. You forced me to.'

'And I've just explained that you cannot prove it. The girl will say what we ask her to say and Beholden and the driver are men of my own.' The voice suddenly hardened, 'And that isn't all. The Admiral had Colonel Russell at gunpoint.'

'I know nothing of his plans for Russell.' The bluster had diminished notably.

'They were to hold him as hostage while we gave him free rein.'

'I didn't know that.'

'I suggest you did.' The bullying counsel's voice came on again. 'I further suggest it was you who thought of it. You went to give aid since you'd thought it up.'

Ben Arie blasphemed which the boss detested, but he thought for some time before he spoke again.

'You don't dare make a public scandal.'

'Don't I? Can you be sure of that? Over your wretched gambling, no, but what you've been doing is to endanger the state.'

Ben Arie said: 'I think you're bluffing.'

'In one sense I confess I am. It would be simpler and cleaner to have you eliminated. A car accident, for instance. Easy.'

'I don't think you'd dare.'

'Are you ready to risk it?'

Ben Arie had begun to shiver; he said and his voice was not quite steady:

'What is your price? I'm not a rich man.'

The boss would have liked to spit but didn't.

'You will resign from the Knesset and leave the party. You will give up all further contact with politics.'

'And if I do not?'

'I told you the choices.'

Ben Arie had begun to weep and the boss looked away at the wall in shame.

'But how am I going to live?'

'That's for you. I believe you were some sort of lawyer once. No respectable lawyer would now give you house-room but there are lawyers who are less than respectable. With such you might find some menial job.'

Ben Arie said through his tears: 'You're cruel.'

'Frankly I have always hated you. I loathe everything a man like you stands for.'

When Ben Arie had gone the boss smiled grimly. He might not have been as urbane as Russell but he'd achieved the same result. Which was victory.

Charles Russell was saying goodbye to Lynne Hammer. When he'd telephoned she hadn't hesitated and now she said briskly:

'Come up and see him. Not the Admiral, he's gone out shopping.'

The big double bed told Russell nothing. It was made up for two and was now half occupied, but not, as Lynne had said, by the Admiral. On one half now stood a carrycot, the baby in it sleeping intently, an act of almost conscious volition. Russell hadn't expected sentiment and Lynne said simply:

'He's a very good baby.' He noticed she didn't fuss with the blankets but she gave the sleeping child a smile. 'Let's have a drink.'

'It's a little early.'

'It's also our last.'

'I'm afraid it almost certainly is.'

A record player was playing softly and Lynne went over and switched it off. 'A favourite of my old man's,' she explained, 'but personally I can't stand that stuff.'

Charles Russell didn't say so but quite agreed. Israelis, or if you preferred the word Jews, were the finest players of strings on earth, but with an eminent and unquestioned exception they needed a non-Jewish conductor, a certain modest Gentile discipline, to keep talent from slipping away into schmaltz. He said none of this but sipped his gin.

Presently Lynne spoke again. 'I'm sorry that this is the end.'

'So am I.'

'But I've gone into this completely. No fooling.' Like the Sheikh she had committed everything but unlike the Sheikh she was wholly contented.

Charles Russell asked softly: 'You think it will last?'

'I'm damned well going to make it last.'

She would, he thought — she had found what she wanted. He rose but she said in surprise:

'Don't go. My old man's at the market — he's sharper than I am.' They might have been together for years. 'I know he'd like to see you.'

'No.'

'Whyever not?'

'I can't explain.'

'Men,' she said, 'are most peculiar.'

'You're fortunate to have had experience.' It was said without a hint of irony. He had never yet left a woman in anger.

Later, in the returning aircraft, the same stewardess came up and smiled. 'Did you have a good time?'

'No, I wouldn't say that.'

'I've heard rumours——'

'You can safely forget them.'

He could see that he'd offended her, much less by his words than by lack of enthusiasm. She asked on a note of sour disapproval:

'So you didn't like Israel?'

'I didn't say that.'

'I know it but it's as clear as can be.' She stared at him. 'Why did you go there?'

'I went there to make up my mind.'

'And did you?'

'No, I'm afraid I didn't.'

She snorted, openly hostile now. Russell was not surprised — he'd learnt that much. It was a hundred per cent for them or nothing. She said with a sudden fierce intensity:

'What did you go to find out?'

'What I felt.'

'About what?'

'I suppose you might call it natural justice.'

She turned on her heel and stalked away.

Natural justice, he thought, as she flounced up the gangway. A very foolish phrase indeed unless you believed it had concrete meaning and in no way could he pretend he did.

But then he had never been good at abstractions.